The 7th Guest

Matthew J. Costello
&
Craig Shaw Gardner

PRIMA PUBLISHING
Rocklin, California

Prima Publishing would like to acknowledge Kellyn Beeck and Jane La Fevre at Trilobyte, as well as Liza Landsman and Merrilee Heifetz at Writers House, for their special assistance on this project.

ISBN: 0-7615-0086-3
Library of Congress Catalog Card Number: 95-069468
Printed in the United States of America
95 96 97 98 AA 10 9 8 7 6 5 4 3 2 1

For Christopher, the last guest in our house.
                                    —Matthew J. Costello

For Tracy, who knows a good game when she sees one.
                                    —Craig Shaw Gardner

ONE

othing kept out the cold. Henry Stauf gathered the remains of his coat around his narrow shoulders. The wind shoved at him, trying to force him to shelter. Here he was, freezing, in a nowhere town halfway between New York City and Lake Ontario. This cold, and it wasn't even winter yet. He seemed to shiver all the time now.

He wished he hadn't thrown away the gun. He was so sure they were going to get him for the stickup after that fat bastard clerk had yanked away his mask.

He had walked into the dusty little store just as the sun was setting, a handkerchief tied to cover all of his face below the eyes. Stauf always planned his robberies for that time of day. It was easier to lose yourself in a hick town like this after it got dark. The place looked like a grocery store, cans and boxes stacked neatly on either side of a long aisle. But Stauf knew the guy ran a speakeasy out of the back room, one of half a dozen such establishments in this town. A speakeasy meant easy money, or so Stauf thought.

As fat as the grocery clerk was, and he must have weighed three hundred pounds, he moved like greased lightning when he saw a man with a mask. The clerk was going for something under the counter, maybe even a gun of his own. But Stauf was even quicker, on top of that clerk before he could make his move. Stauf demanded money, and booze besides, sure that the clerk wouldn't dare argue with Stauf's gun.

But Stauf pointed the gun away from the clerk for an instant as he scooped up the money. And the clerk, jowels quivering, two beady, fearful eyes set deep in his fleshy face, jumped forward and pulled away the mask.

Stauf panicked, then, running with the fistful of bills in his hand, forgetting about the three bottles of hooch he'd set on the counter. Panicked and threw away the gun.

He'd used that gun plenty of times before. Pointed it at people, made them give him their money, their jewelry, just about any damn thing he wanted, really. He'd only fired it once, and that time kind of by accident: the time he had to wave the piece at that smart-ass attendant at a filling station. When the bullet went through the attendant's shoulder, it took the smile right off his face.

At the store, he panicked because he wanted to use the gun again. When the clerk yanked down the handkerchief covering Stauf's face, Henry had a picture of what came next. He'd put the cold muzzle of his .44 up against the clerk's nose and squeeze the trigger, just once, gentle as a kiss. Stauf wanted to watch the clerk's blood and bone spatter across the fat cheeks to either side. He wanted to hear the clerk's scream cut short by a bullet in the brain.

You kill somebody, they send you up for life.

Stauf heard those words, like there was a little voice in the back of his head. Killing was different from stealing. Stauf stole because it was easy, he stole because he needed the money, he stole because he'd never been caught. And if he was caught, the hick cops in these dumb-ass burgs would nail him for one or two jobs at most, strictly short time stuff. But he wasn't ready for murder.

So he dumped the gun and ran, thinking next time he looked at some guy's smug face he'd pull the trigger for sure.

It wasn't the first time that he had heard those voices talking to him. They were never more than a whisper in his head, and sometimes they were little more than an insistent thought. Listening to those little voices had kept Stauf alive.

At least until this cold fall night. Now he was stuck at the edge of some godforsaken little town two miles this side of nowhere. He wasn't any good unless he had a drink or two under his belt, and could feel the warmth that liquor gave him in his gut and in his blood. And he couldn't remember the last time he'd had a decent meal. He'd walked until he couldn't walk any farther. Then he'd fallen down and slept away the day.

Somehow, Stauf managed to get back on his feet. He glanced up at the clear, cold night sky. The stars were so bright he had to look away. He'd fallen asleep in that lot full of crabgrass and half-dead trees that the locals called a park. What the hell was the name of this place, anyway? He couldn't remember. Right now, he couldn't think of much of anything except how the wind froze his insides, and how good a gun would feel in his hand.

Stauf couldn't stop anybody without a gun. He didn't have a gun. Maybe he had enough left in his fists to do a decent job, if he snuck up on somebody. And if he could stop his hands from shaking.

Stauf stuffed his hands in his coat pockets. His right knuckles hit something.

He must have put something in his pocket before he'd fallen asleep. Stauf tried to get his shaking fingers to pull it out, thinking maybe it was a forgotten bottle or the last bites of a sandwich. He had stolen something from a grocery, but he couldn't remember if that had been hours or days ago. But the thing in his pocket was hard and cold under his fingers, more like wood than glass.

He got his hand around it at last and pulled it free, holding it up to the light of the stars.

It was a hammer.

He remembered now. About noon time, he'd wandered by a house under constrution. The builders were all eating lunch on the far side of the place. For a second, he'd thought about begging for food. But the cops didn't like that. They'd already taken Stauf down to the station once, giving him a good beating after he asked a woman for a dime. Nobody begged in their town. Stauf didn't think he'd survive another one of their beatings.

But, while the builders were all eating lunch out of sight, they'd left their tools behind. Maybe Stauf couldn't beg, but he could steal.

He saw the hammer then—a small one that fit nicely in his hand. The voices had told him to take it. The voices were sorry he'd thrown away his gun. They wanted him to have a weapon.

It felt good to have something in his hand.

Stauf heard a woman's voice. Outside his head this time. She was singing, "Bringing in the sheaves, bringing in the sheaves, we will come rejoicing . . ."

A woman, walking through the park, probably coming back from choir practice from that church down the street. Thought she'd take a little stroll on such a fine, clear night. Stauf stepped away from the path, back into the trees. He swung the hammer. It gave him strength. The woman's voice was getting louder. Coming back from church. People often wore their nicest things when they went to church, especially the women, trotting out the good jewelry for the faithful to see.

"—bringing in the sheaves."

She'd pass right in front of him.

He'd wait for the voices to tell him when.

"Bringing in the sheaves," she began all over again, singing the words more loudly now, as if the hymn would protect her against the night. Her voice was strong, as if she was used to singing, but her voice quavered a bit on the high notes, as if they were hard to reach in the cold night air.

The hammer felt warm in Stauf's hand. It felt good to hold onto something solid; solid like a gun. Stauf smiled at the thought. No hymn was going to protect anybody tonight.

She stepped into sight, a short woman in a long black coat, her purse clutched close by her side. Her hard-soled shoes clacked against the concrete path, giving a rhythm to her song.

"—We will come rejoicing—"

Now!

The voices threw him forward, out from the shadows of the trees, hammer raised above his head. He rushed toward the woman, his tired legs somehow managing a ragged run. His ears were filled with the sound of his heart and his own breathing, making the woman's song seem very far away.

She turned and stared at him open-eyed.

He raised the hammer even higher, ready to strike her down.

But the woman didn't look afraid.

"Oh," she whispered, "you poor man."

She pitied him. The way he shivered and could barely walk, his threadbare coat and pants. She felt sorry for him.

She was looking down on him.

She reached out a hand, as if she wanted to give him something with those pudgy fingers. Give poor Stauf a little something, a crumb or two; he can't take care of himself. Give him a little something before you kick him around again. She looked like she was trying to smile. Everybody smiled down at Stauf.

Stauf felt the rage well up inside him.

No one would look down at him ever again.

All his rage was in his hammer. His arm was lightning, the hammer thunder.

He hit her in the head. He could feel her skull crush as the hammer sank into something soft underneath.

She grunted in pain.

"Not enough!" he shouted back. He had to punish her, punish all of them, for looking down at him, laughing at him, beating him, throwing him away like yesterday's garbage. He raised the hammer above his head and hit her again. And again.

He didn't want her pity. He wanted to hear her scream.

She fell to the path instead. Fell there and lay still. He stood for a moment and watched her blood spread across the concrete, a dark pool that flowed out from her head in an expanding halo.

Then he grabbed her purse and fled.

Two

There was no kindness behind their smiles. Their words were polite and their expressions pleasant, but Edward Knox couldn't look them in the eyes. If he hadn't been able to tell by their large size, with their cheap ready-made suits doing nothing to hide their heavily muscled frames, the emptiness of their gazes gave them away. They were Whitey Chester's men. They were there to do a job. And nothing Edward Knox could say would change that.

They had been waiting for him in his kitchen when he got home from work. With their size and impatient manner, they dominated the compact kitchen of Knox's small and tidy house. Small and tidy, just the right size for Knox and his wife, with a bright white kitchen just barely large enough for sink and stove and icebox, and a little breakfast nook across the way. Somehow, these coarse men in their dark suits seemed too large to fit in such a cozy space.

The back door was open. Knox imagined the lock had been forced. Somehow, it didn't seem proper to examine the damage while the two men were here.

At least his wife was nowhere around. He guessed he should thank the Lord for small favors. No matter what these two wanted to do, maybe he could at least protect his beloved Elinor for a little while longer.

The men had told Knox to sit, and he thought it best not to argue. They then proceeded to quickly, politely, and perhaps a bit too eagerly describe what was going to happen if he didn't pay. If he didn't pay? He couldn't even begin to find that kind of money. If only he could get these men to understand!

He could hear the desperation in his own voice as he tried to reason with them. "But how can I pay you if you break my hand?"

The slightly larger of the two men, who had said that his name was Bert, smiled at his objection. "I'm glad you asked, Mr. Knox." He glanced at his co-worker, who hardly spoke at all and, from the lack of introduction, apparently didn't have a name, either.

"See," Bert continued, "Mr. Chester wants you to understand the nature of our business. Breaking your hand might be unfortunate for all concerned—"

He paused, and his nameless friend nodded sadly.

"—but it may also be necessary," Bert continued. His friend's nod became even more vigorous. "That kind of a loss here, as unfortunate as it may be, will send a real message to our other customers. You might not be able to pay, but others will."

"Yeah," his friend agreed. Knox didn't like the enthusiasm he heard in that single word.

Bert slapped Knox's shoulder gently, like they were a couple of old pals. "Hey, you'll find a way to pay." It was Bert's turn to nod at his nameless friend. "If not, we'll break your other hand. And then both your legs."

His friend's grin got bigger with every passing word. Knox half expected the big man to giggle.

In comparison, Bert's smile was the very picture of restraint. "And when we're done with you, we'll start on your wife."

Oh, no. They could do what they wanted to Knox, but he couldn't allow anything to happen to Elinor. He looked away from the two bruisers, afraid to show too much emotion.

"Mr. Knox, when you borrow money from Mr. Chester and don't pay on time, well, it can turn into a lifetime commitment." Bert sighed. "If you gotta sell pencils on the street corner, you're gonna raise the money."

His friend opened his mouth to agree. "We're gonna be around for a long, long time."

This all seemed a little unreal. Knox had always given his wife the finest things he could afford. And sometimes, even things he couldn't quite afford. Perhaps lately, with his wife's delicate nature, and the small illnesses that seemed to come on both of them as they grew older, he had spent a little bit too much on his wife's happiness. Somehow, he had found himself thousands of dollars in debt.

He had tried the ponies to solve his problems, but not a single horse had come in. And the money he'd borrowed from the company payroll was sure to be missed any day. Knox hadn't even wanted to begin to think about what might happen if that discrepancy was discovered.

There had been nothing left but to float a little short-term loan. The fellows down at the speakeasy told him about Mr. Chester. His rates were a little high, but he didn't ask any questions. That suited Knox just fine. He would get the money back into the payroll account with a minimum of fuss. After all, his fortunes would be turning around any day.

But his luck had gotten no better. The horses were just as slow. And he didn't dare touch the payroll again.

Knox had heard these gentlemen could be a little insistent about repayment. But he never imagined it would be anything like this.

The mostly silent partner reached out towards Knox. His fingers snapped, as if hungry for Knox's hand.

"Just a few hours," Knox heard himself say.

Bert shook his head slowly. "Mr. Knox, you're a nice old geezer, but we've spent too much time with you already." His voice took on a tired tone, as if he'd said these words too many times before. "We're getting behind in our other obligations."

Other obligations? Knox wondered how many hands they broke on an average day.

"We'd need a reason," the nameless friend added, his own hand an inch away from closing around Knox's wrist. "Or we do it now."

Reason? Knox felt the panic well up inside him. He couldn't think of the reason why he was here, or the reason why these men would break his hands. What was the reason for anything?

He pulled his hands back, hugging them close to his suit jacket.

He felt the envelope in his pocket.

"Oh, yes." He quickly pulled the invitation free. "Here's where the money's coming from. In just a few more hours."

He opened the envelope and offered Bert the registered letter he'd received at his office earlier in the day.

"Maybe we can just break a finger," the nameless friend said hopefully. "You can still do most anything with a broken finger."

But Bert took the letter from Knox and opened it. He seemed to read it all in a single glance.

Bert whistled. "The richest man in town, huh?"

It was Knox's turn to nod, his head bobbing up and down so quickly it threatened to make him dizzy. "Yes, old Mr. Stauf. He has nothing to do with his money, now that his toy shop is closed. And you can see he thinks highly of me."

Bert scowled at that. The other man looked back to Bert, as if waiting for some sign that it was time to break things.

"I have more than just his ear!" Knox added quickly. "Mr. Stauf is very interested in my plans. Very interested—and very rich."

Bert's frown deepened, as if it hurt to make this kind of decision. "Well, maybe Mr. Chester can give you a little more time after all."

"We hate to have unhappy customers," the other man added. But he kept staring at Knox's hands.

Knox continued to nod. Maybe Stauf would float him a loan. If not, he had heard the house was full of antiques. Maybe he could manage to borrow one or two of those, too.

He offered to show the two men the door.

"No, thanks," Bert answered. "We've already found it once."

"We'll be seeing you, Mr. Knox," his friend added. "Right after the party."

With that, they were gone. Knox clutched the invitation, and the short, personal note that had accompanied it, as if it was the only thing in the world that might keep him whole and healthy . . . which it was.

He was still sitting at the kitchen table when his wife appeared half an hour later, with a story about how she had received a message from her Uncle Phil to meet her at the drugstore downtown. Knox had always urged Elinor to be nice to Uncle Phil. He was her one relative with money.

Except her uncle had never sent any such message. He hadn't been at the drugstore, and when Elinor had called his house, the cook had said that he was out of town.

Knox guessed that little deception had been a gift from Bert and his friend, to get Elinor out of the way. He was glad they had at least spared her that unpleasantness.

But he couldn't let his wife see how upset he'd become. She depended upon him so. He looked down at the invitation, still cradled in his hands.

"Dear," he began, looking up at her with his best smile. "Something happened today, something that I think might be very rewarding."

He handed her the invitation.

She screamed when she touched the envelope, throwing it to the floor as if it burned her hand.

Knox jumped from the chair and rushed to her side.

"Dear?" he asked. She should have been pleased, perhaps overjoyed. He had never expected a reaction like this.

"Oh. Edward. I don't know." She stared down at the envelope, her arms folded before her chest as if she might ward off a chill. "There was something about where this has been, who's touched the paper—" She paused as if the resonance had taken her words away.

Knox took her in his arms. She started to cry. Elinor was such a sensitive woman. This day, with the false errand, must have been very trying for her. She was having one of her "spells," as she called them. They always made her very emotional. Knox could never quite understand them.

He looked down at the white envelope, very bright against the dull brown linoleum of their kitchen floor. It was only a party. What could his wife have possibly felt, just by touching an envelope?

Edward Knox sighed. It had been a *very* trying day, indeed.

THREE

Stauf half-ran, half-stumbled across the park. He had no idea where to go, only that he had to get away.

The ground sucked at the bottom of his shoes. The once dry earth had turned to mud. He staggered to a halt and looked up at where his feet had taken him. He had ventured into the marshland next to the lake that ran along the edge of town.

The cold air felt like ice in his lungs. He still couldn't get enough of it, breathing in ragged gasps. Now that he'd stopped, he didn't think he'd ever get his feet to move again. He looked down at his hands. One held the purse, the other the bloody hammer.

He looked out at the lake again. Maybe the voices had brought him here. The water was stagnant in this corner of the lake, full of weeds and dead leaves. Nobody would think of looking for a hammer here.

His body swayed as he swung the hammer, as if throwing the bloody tool away would be too much for his balance. He let the hammer go anyway. He staggered, but somehow managed to stay on his feet. The tool made a satisfying splash as it disappeared beneath the still water.

Stauf opened the purse. There wasn't much inside: tissues, a comb, a small cosmetic mirror. They all followed the hammer into the lake. He pulled out a small change purse, the kind that held together with a metal clasp. He popped the clasp open and pulled out the contents, six neatly folded one-dollar bills.

This was not at all what he was hoping for. The woman had been wearing a nice cloth coat. She had had her hair done and her shoes looked new. This was barely enough for a night or two of drinking. He had killed somebody for this?

He had killed somebody. Stauf took another deep breath. There was finally enough air in his lungs. He had killed somebody, and the night was still stone cold and quiet. No screams, no shouts, no sirens, no dogs. Nobody seemed to care where Stauf was or what he'd done. Maybe the killing didn't make any difference.

He had killed somebody, and it hadn't felt bad at all.

The voices hadn't warned him away this time. Whether he had a gun or a hammer or nothing but his bare hands, maybe he was meant to kill. Maybe the voices had just wanted him to wait until he was ready. Maybe now they were telling him he was beyond the law.

Or maybe, Stauf thought, he just needed a drink.

Stauf shoved the money in his coat pocket. The promise of a couple of stiff belts got his feet moving again. He turned to his left and followed the edge of the lake until he found a street. He turned left again, back toward town, hoping it wasn't too far to the nearest speakeasy.

He put his hand in his pocket to feel the crisp one-dollar bills. He liked the feel of money, wanted a lot more of it around him. Just resting his hands against those bills made him feel better.

It had been so easy, and so quick, back there in the park. And it had felt so satisfying to crush her skull.

"Hey!" a voice, a human voice, shouted almost in his ear. "You!"

Stauf leapt back from the road, turning toward the noise with a speed he didn't know he had in him. He was so lost in what he'd done, he hadn't even heard the police car pull up next to him.

The cop inside the wagon had his gun pointed straight at Stauf's head.

"You wouldn't be thinking about trying to run, would you?" the cop said with a wave of his revolver.

Stauf shook his head, trying to catch his breath all over again. The cop's shout had almost stopped his heart.

Gun still on Stauf, the cop climbed out of the car and opened the back door. The policeman waved Stauf inside.

"You are Henry Stauf," the cop said, a statement, not a question. "A couple of the boys described you from the last time you were at the station. We like to know every stranger who passes through town." The cop smiled. "We make sure they don't wear out their welcome."

Stauf climbed in the car. His ribs were still sore from a few days ago, when the cops had worked him over for public begging. He didn't want to think what they'd do to him for murder.

The policeman slammed the door after him and climbed back behind the wheel. They drove in silence, back in to town.

Stauf's head was silent, too. The voices had been coming to him more often than ever lately, sometimes two and three times a day. Where were they when he really needed them?

The streets were dark and deserted as they sped back towards the police station. They passed row after row of well-kept houses, all with new paint and nicely mowed lawns, and hardly any with even a light in the window. Most of the people kept to themselves and went to bed early in a place like this. The perfect small town—right now, Henry Stauf wished he was anyplace other then here.

The cop jerked the car to a halt in front of the station. Stauf was yanked from the back seat and hurried up the steps. He expected to be taken back to one of the cells, like before. Someplace quiet, where no one could hear what was being done.

Instead, he was dumped in the corner of a large office full people, about half of them in uniform. The cop that brought him in yelled at him not to move, then turned to face a beefy Sergeant sitting at a large oak desk.

"I got him," the first cop said with a self-satisfied nod. He chuckled as he waved at Stauf. "The guy who robbed Sweeny's Grocery."

Stauf looked up at that. They had arrested him for the grocery store? That was nothing. He'd grabbed a loaf of bread and some beef jerky, then managed to stumble out before the grocer could get his fat ass out from behind the counter. That had happened days ago; Stauf had almost forgotten about it.

The Sergeant grimaced in Stauf's direction. From the look on his face, he didn't like what he smelled. Stauf looked away from the cops. He didn't want to show them how relieved he felt.

"We've seen this guy before, haven't we?" the Sergeant asked. "Listen, Henretty, we got something worse. There's been a murder."

The hope that had started to flutter around in Stauf's chest froze and died. He remembered how the cops had used their nightsticks on him before. They beat you until you'd admit to anything. Once they got him back in that quiet cell, they'd start with the grocery store and work their way up to murder.

"Greta Schultz," the Sergeant went on. "Walking through the park on her way home from choir practice."

Stauf found himself looking back at the cops, as if his eyes could do nothing else.

"Mrs. Schultz?" Henretty asked, his voice rising in disbelief. "From St. Luke's?" In a small town like this, Stauf realized, they knew everybody who went to choir practice. In a small town like this, they knew everything about everybody.

"She wouldn't hurt—" Henretty went on. The pride that had been in his voice was replaced by a cold fury. "Who would do—" He turned back to look at Stauf.

Stauf still couldn't look away. Henretty knew.

"It would be easy to pin the murder on this guy," the Sergeant agreed. "Except he isn't the only vagrant passing through town. When Townsend found the body, he also found a fella trying to steal Mrs. Schultz's coat."

"Hell, he killed her for a coat?" Henretty leaned on the Sergeant's desk. "Mrs. Schultz, huh? We got this guy?"

The Sergeant nodded.

"When we question him, I want a piece."

The Sergeant showed his teeth at that. "Everybody in the station's gonna want to be back in that cell."

Henretty slammed a fist down on the desk. He turned back to Stauf. "Well, let's see if we can give this bread snatcher some accommodations before we get down to the real business."

The Sergeant ordered Stauf to empty his pockets. The only thing he had were the six folded dollar bills.

Henretty stared at the bills in amazement. "This bum actually has money?"

"Uh—" Stauf said quickly, the words coming into his head as if someone else was speaking them. "I managed to do some odd jobs."

Henretty laughed. "Jobs? You?"

Stauf nodded, letting the words pour out again. "I can still manage to swing a hammer."

The Sergeant grunted at that. "Maybe this money will pay for the things you stole. Judge will go easy on you."

Somehow, Stauf found he was smiling.

"We'll see how happy you are after you spend a couple of days in jail," Henretty said as he yanked Stauf to his feet. "Come on. Let's get you out of here. I got important business to attend to."

They gave him a cell at the far end of the hallway from the place he'd been questioned before. As he fell asleep, he could hear a faint pounding and the occasional scream.

He tried to get comfortable on the wooden slab that served as a bed. The business down the hall didn't have anything to do with him. He knew now he was meant for greater things.

That night, in his dreams, the distant screams turned to voices, and the voices sang to him in his cell.

FOUR

Brian Dutton woke up at the edge of the bed, already sitting, as if poised to run away.

No matter how many times he had the dream, it never got any easier. He always woke up short of breath, heart pounding as if he had just run a mile. The bedclothes were tangled and drenched with perspiration. Funny how he could sweat so much when the dream was so cold.

The dream was with him still. He saw the face pressed up against the ice, his brother's face. And in that expression, that sad resignation in the mouth and eyes, Brian could see his brother Kevin's unmistakable knowledge that his life was over.

Brian threw the bedclothes aside and got out of bed. He needed to walk around, maybe get a drink of water, give the image of Kevin a chance to leave his mind.

As if Kevin would ever leave him.

Brian had never been a match for Kevin. His older brother had been a better ball player and a better student. Girls flocked to him, neighbors laughed at his jokes, dogs wanted to be his lifelong friend. He was their parents' favorite, too, one year older and one step better than his brother. It was the way of the world, and Brian had to accept it.

At least he did until that terrible day out on the ice. It had started out pretty much as usual for the brothers Dutton. Brian had enough trouble simply staying up on his skates. But Kevin's skates acted like extensions of his legs. Once he got going, he could race with the wind.

Brian was doing his best to remain standing, keeping close to the pond's edge, hoping for a snowdrift to cushion his next fall. Kevin was swooping toward the center of the pond, doing great circles and figure eights. Next thing, Brian swore, his brother would be skating numbers that hadn't even been invented.

Maybe they shouldn't have been skating that day. Even though it was still January, it was unseasonably warm for the second day in a row. One of those midwinter thaws you get upstate, a teasing bit of spring before being plunged back into two more months of winter.

But on a day like that, you had to go outside, you had to move. The snow was too deep and crusty for running. So the only way for the brothers to move was to skate.

Kevin and Brian had risen early and gone out to the lake on the edge of town before most of their friends had even sat down to breakfast. They were the only people on the lake shore that morning. The sun rising above the hills turned the sky the color of blood.

"Come on, Brian!" Kevin called, already a couple of dozen yards away.

"I'm coming!" Brian had yelled back, even though he didn't want to leave the relative security of the shore behind. He wished he had the confidence to zoom across the ice. He wished, just once, he could be better than his brother at something.

And then Kevin screamed. Brian could hear the ice crack beneath his brother's skates. The thaw had thinned the ice. It could no longer support Kevin's weight.

Kevin cried for help, arms flailing, as the ice opened and he sank. He grabbed for the nearest edge of solid ice, but it crumbled in his hands.

Brian skated towards his brother as fast as he could. But it wasn't fast enough. And how could he hope to get close enough to do anything for his brother without the ice failing under him? It wouldn't do either of them any good if he fell in, too.

"Brian!" Kevin called. "Do something—I can't—so cold—"

But Brian stopped skating abruptly, a single thought filling his head.

Kevin could never be better than Brian again, if Kevin were dead.

Brian shook himself. He didn't have time for that kind of nonsense. He looked back to shore. Maybe he could find a tree branch or something and reach out to his brother that way, pulling him out of the water onto the thicker ice closer to shore.

But Brian could no longer hear Kevin's cries. He turned back out toward the lake again, in time to watch his brother's open hand sink below the surface.

Then, Brian skated out towards his brother, going faster than he had ever thought possible. He called Kevin's name, but got no answer. He stopped, half a dozen feet from the edge of the crack. There, wedged between two plates of ice, was his brother's brown parka. And, just below that, pressed against a piece of translucent ice, staring up from beneath the waves, was his brother's face.

Kevin was dead. But Kevin was still with him. He kept coming back to haunt Brian's dreams.

Maybe, Brian had thought a hundred, perhaps a thousand times, if he hadn't stopped, he might have been able to save his brother. But at other moments, he knew that the instant he paused not only saved his life, but gave his life a whole new direction.

His parents could never forget what had happened—and they didn't let Brian forget either. "If only Kevin were still alive," they'd say. But now Brian got on the team, dated the girls, got the money to go to college. With the hope of the family gone, everybody had to pay some attention to Brian.

Over time, Brian realized that his brother had taught him a valuable lesson. Sometimes, in life, you had to be ruthless. You had to look out for number one. Sometimes he thought, the others will never do better than me, if they're dead.

Not that he was a murderer. But in the business world there was more than one way to kill your opponent. He had managed to start up a neat little manufacturing base underselling the competition. Maybe his wares weren't quite as good as other brands, but if he sold them cheap enough for long enough, the other brands would eventually die off.

No matter what, Brian had learned to be a survivor. Kevin had been the favored one once, but now that Kevin was gone, Brian was a lucky man.

Or so he told himself. But his business success was too small and too slow; one small factory in one small town. Half of his big deals fell through; the others hardly made a difference. He worked and worked and still barely managed to stay afloat.

The only real success story in their town was Henry Stauf. Everybody had to have his toys. There seemed to be no end to the demand.

And then, one day, Stauf simply stopped making them.

What was the man, crazy? If Stauf had tired of producing the products, he should let somebody else take over— someone like Brian Dutton. He could bring the same assembly-line production to Stauf's toys that he had to his other products. The toys might not be as personalized, but Brian could open new factories to meet the demand.

This is what he should be dreaming about, not his long-dead brother. If only his brother would leave him alone!

Sometimes, Brian Dutton wondered if his brother was waiting for Brian to join him, that maybe it was time for

Brian to die, too. Except, even there, Kevin had died in a much more spectacular way than Brian ever could.

Enough about his brother! Brian walked into the other room and looked down at the letter spread open on the dining room table. Stauf wouldn't send him an invitation without a reason.

Brian was the survivor. Brian was the lucky one. Stauf was a wealthy man. Stauf needed to do something with all that money.

Brian had taken over for Kevin, once. Maybe now he could take over for Stauf.

FIVE

A week later, they let Stauf out of jail.

His trial had been short and sweet. Stauf had pled guilty, and said that he'd seen the error of his ways. That was what the voices told him to do. It was quick, it was simple, and it seemed to please the judge no end.

The judge, an old man who had trouble hearing the evidence, ordered that the grocer receive the six dollars Stauf had on him. "Restitution for stolen merchandise," the judge called it. His Honor had given Stauf the week in jail, less time served, and punctuated his sentence with a sharp rap of his gavel. The old man had looked over his thick glasses and told Stauf that once his jail time was done, he had two options: find another job or get out of town. The judge said he knew times were hard, but if Stauf tried anything else, times would get harder still.

Stauf nodded as he stared at the floor. He glanced at his scuffed shoes, his rumpled pants that hung so loosely on his too-thin frame. It was important to be humble. The voices had been very explicit on this point. He had to be the model prisoner and spend as little time in jail as possible. He had to be free for the real work to begin.

Stauf wondered what the real work would be. Not that it mattered. He had been alone for so long, the voices were a real comfort. He'd do anything to keep them around.

So he cooled his heels in jail. There were worse places to spend cold autumn nights. And he didn't even have to worry about that business with the choir lady. It would never go to trial. After two days of questioning, the other vagrant had hung himself in his cell. At least that's what the police said. Case closed.

Then the week was up and Stauf was free.

The voices had been quiet after the trial, giving him four days of loneliness behind bars. Once or twice, sitting alone in his cell, he had wondered if he had heard them at all. But no, he felt sure they would come back when he needed them.

Now though—now that he saw the sun rather than the walls of a cell—he expected to hear the voices again at any moment. But the only sounds here were outside his head, everyday noises like birds and dogs and cars. It was surprisingly warm in the sun, an Indian Summer day, and Stauf felt like taking a walk.

After a while, he realized he was striding very purposefully through town. He took a right turn, walked down a block, then took a left. Maybe, he thought, the voices were telling him what to do after all. His feet were taking him somewhere.

He turned another corner and found himself in front of the construction site, the same place where he'd gotten the hammer. It was mid-morning, and the workers were crawling all over the building, hammering and shouting and making all kinds of noise.

Was he here for another hammer?

Somehow, that didn't feel right. A bricklayer glared at Stauf like he didn't belong here. Stauf strolled away from the suspicious workman, walking easily down the path that ran along one edge of the building site.

He wondered if he should leave and come back like before, when the workers were busy with lunch. With any luck, he could have his choice of tools. But the only thing he knew was that his feet didn't want to stop. He had to keep on walking.

Something shone on the path ahead of him, shimmering in the sun like a precious gem. This was why he was here. Stauf knew it the moment it caught his eye.

He glanced casually from side to side. At the moment no workers were visible at this end of the building, but Stauf didn't want to call any attention to himself. As much as he wanted to hurry, Stauf kept his pace steady.

He stopped at last, his feet almost touching his prize. There, in the grass next to a new cement walkway, was a knife, the metal blade shining in the sun.

A knife. So much cleaner than a hammer, so much quieter than a gun. Stauf had been brought here for this. The voices knew.

He knelt and picked it up. The handle fit nicely in his hand, as if it had been made just for him. The blade was short but very sharp. It looked like a most efficient tool.

He stood, and his feet started to move again.

It seemed inevitable that his steps would lead him back to the park. Where else was there to go?

He came to that place in the park where he had met the woman singing hymns and hit her with his hammer. He remembered it all as if it had happened only a moment ago: the look on her face, the swing of his arm, the feel of metal hitting bone. And all, all for the voices. For an instant, he wished he could do it all again.

It was easy enough to find the exact spot. The sidewalk still held a purplish stain where the woman's head had hit the pavement. He could remember looking down at her still figure, the blood framing her head like some dark halo.

Stauf looked up at the blue sky and listened to the noises of the park, noises even louder than before. It seemed that all the birds and dogs and screaming children were making as much of a commotion as they knew how, as if all that sound might keep summer around for one more day.

Fat chance. Children never got what they wanted. Stauf certainly hadn't. All he could remember was his father hitting him, because little Henry hadn't done his chores, or had talked too loud, or had been in the room when his father hit his mother. Just about any reason—or no reason at all—would get him a sharp slap across the head, then a second cuff, going the other way, until his head was so dizzy and sore little Henry could barely stand.

But Stauf didn't want to think about little Henry any more, or the way the beatings hurt, or how scared he felt, or what little Henry wanted to do to his father. He wasn't little Henry any more. He gripped the knife so hard his palm hurt. Little Henry didn't have a knife, nor a hammer. Little Henry didn't have the voices.

But where *were* the voices? His feet had stopped at last, and he still heard nothing. He shivered, feeling the chill that lurked behind this last warm day.

Stauf suddenly wanted a drink. It had been a week, after all; he was amazed his body could have gone so long without alcohol. He knew of a place not too far from here, a little gin joint on the alley off Main Street. But the judge had taken away his six dollars. How would he get a drink when he had no money?

He could think of nothing but the knife. The wooden handle felt warm in his palm. At last, this was a sign.

He looked up, and there was a glow in the air before him. It appeared suddenly, as if someone had thrown a switch, but the glow was much too bright for a simple lightbulb. The white hot blaze looked more like a miniature sun. Stauf walked toward the light; and the answer he'd been looking for.

At the center of that glow was a small figure, only slightly bigger than his hand. At first Stauf thought the figure was human. But then he realized it was only shaped like a human female, like a little girl. The thing in the light was a doll.

It had been carved from wood with great skill and an eye for detail, with movable joints at elbow and knee and fine lines to show fingers and toes. But the most extraordinary thing about the doll was its face. Its eyes seemed to stare straight at Stauf, maybe even straight through him. He felt as if he was being judged, as if he was faced with a choice. If he didn't choose correctly, he might lose the voices forever.

But the feeling went even deeper than that. There was no way he could look away. Stauf had known this face before.

Perhaps it was the face of his mother, always hiding behind her tears. Or the wife who had left Stauf long ago, gone one night while he slept, leaving behind nothing but an empty bed. Or the woman who had fallen dead on this spot, her song stilled forever. Stauf stared deep into the face. And the doll stared silently back, refusing to give up its secrets.

Somehow, the doll's face was none of those women, and all of them at the same time. It was as if the face was already a part of him, just like the voices in his head.

With that thought, the light flew away, darting like a firefly toward the trees. Stauf ran to follow. He had to look into that face again. He needed to understand.

The light sank to earth before him and came to rest over a thick piece of wood, the remains of a branch fallen from one of the trees. And as Stauf stared down at the light he saw inside the branch.

There, deep within, was the doll. And the doll was calling for Henry to let it out.

At last, Henry Stauf knew what the knife was for.

Six

artine Burden slammed the door.

She had seen that mailman smirking at her. As if she should only answer the door when she was fully dressed, and ready to go out on the town. So she had opened the door wearing her housecoat; it was an elegant, black silk kimono, after all, far finer than the dowdy flowered dresses most of the women wore around here. That kimono was one of the few nice things she had kept from her time with Siegfried. And why should she care?

She didn't know what that mailman expected from her.

Or perhaps she did. He hadn't been able to keep his eyes off her. Even behind his thick glasses, she could see his gaze wander over her, from her beautiful, long dark hair—not quite the style of the day, but she couldn't bear to cut it—down to her petite brocade slippers. She still had her figure; that was one more thing Siegfried hadn't managed to take. And she looked very good in black silk; it made her fair skin look like ivory, and heightened the deep green of her eyes.

But it was only when the postman pushed forward a clipboard and asked her to sign for the registered letter that she took any real interest in the mousy little man.

She quickly signed the line he pointed to and snatched the envelope away from his prying gaze. She did reward him with the slightest of smiles and a softspoken "thank you."

The mailman simply stood there and stared. She often had that effect on men.

So she pushed the door shut in his face.

Martine allowed herself the slightest of smiles. From the mailman's reaction, she still had what it took to get somewhere in this world.

As if she had really gotten anyplace. Martine Burden, occupant of one of the finest furnished rooms in town. Half of her wanted to laugh, while the other half wanted to scream.

Instead, she turned back to the front door and looked out of the small frosted pane cut toward the top of the door to let in a bit of light. The postman had turned and was walking away slowly, as if he was in a daze. As he walked he shook his head, back and forth, back and forth, perhaps to clear his simple mind after the shocking thing he'd seen: that provocatively dressed woman he'd gab about to every soul in town.

Something inside Martine wanted to call the mailman back and give him something to really talk about.

But the impulse was gone almost as soon as it entered her head. Why bother? Maybe answering the door at two in the afternoon in this sort of attire wasn't as respectable as some in town would like. But what was there to get dressed for in a town like this?

She turned away and walked down the worn hallway carpet, so bare in spots you could see the floorboards through the pale blue fibers, back towards her corner room. Martine Burden, living once again in her old home town. Not that anyone here wanted to see her anymore.

She had come back here because this was all she knew. But her mother, not to mention most of her old friends, wouldn't even talk to her. She had gone to New York City and put on airs. And with a foreign man besides! It made no difference that Siegfried was royalty. Or at least he had said he was; everyone in the big city was so much more respectful if your first name was preceded by a title.

So what if she had been fooled by him, fooled and then deserted? No explanations were allowed, and no sympathy should be expected. Those few around town who would talk to Martine only wanted to remind her, over and over again, of all the wrong she had done. They would let her back into their good graces only if she admitted the depth of her sin. To live among these fine church-going people, she would have to crawl and beg for forgiveness.

She'd spit the forgiveness back in their faces.

She looked down at the envelope still clutched in her hands. This letter was the first interesting thing that had happened in weeks. She grabbed the letter opener from the top of her cluttered bureau and carefully slit the envelope's top. Inside was an invitation to a party that weekend at the Stauf mansion. And there was another sheet of paper enclosed, as well, fine vellum filled with flowing script, a personal note, just for her. A personal note, by registered mail? Maybe somebody in this town valued her company after all.

Not so long ago, she had gone to fine parties like this every night, the fiancée of a European count, half of a couple that was asked everywhere in New York society. Men bowed to her and kissed her hand. And every young beau in the room would demand a dance. They'd dance and laugh and drink until dawn, night after night, a constant whirl with no end in sight.

Until the night she returned to her hotel and found that the management had locked her out of her room. Nonpayment of rent, they said. All of her belongings had been seized; all she had left were the contents of her purse, a party dress, and one thin shawl.

At first, she had thought it was some sort of misunderstanding. Siegfried had always taken care of everything. Surely, he had simply forgotten to transfer some funds to the proper account.

But Siegfried no longer occupied the room across the hall. The management informed her he had vacated the hotel, and taken his accounts with him.

Martine had found Siegfried easily enough; in its way, New York society was incredibly small. She spotted him outside the new hotel, another woman on his arm.

He made a date with her when she demanded it, for old times' sake, he said. And, once they were alone, he had laughed at her. What did she think she was? he asked. Nothing but a trophy, to be shown to society. Martine was pretty enough, but she had no connections. He needed a better trophy, and his new woman, Susan, came from one of the finest families in town. It was all a matter of money, after all.

Martine was devastated. She had told the hotel staff a story that was pretty close to the truth, embellished with a few tears. A sympathetic assistant manager had managed to get her a suitcase full of her belongings: a suitcase, where once she had had half a dozen steamer trunks.

She had been a fool, following a count from a country she had never even heard of. Now she doubted that the place even existed.

And, once Siegfried had left her, society didn't want anything to do with her either. Men smiled apologetically as their gaze shifted elsewhere, women gossiped behind their fans, maître'd's could no longer find her a table, doormen looked through her as if she wasn't there.

So she had brought her only suitcase back here, to this tiny town she thought she had escaped forever.

Of course, she had sold off a few of her things just to live. But she had kept a few of the fine things as well, things from a world she had belonged to, at least for a few short weeks. She had enough left to get dressed again for this fancy party. Especially a party at the Stauf Mansion. From what she heard, Stauf was the richest man in town.

And she guessed he was in ill health, too. The way rumors flew around this burg, some had said he was already dead. She actually laughed aloud at that. From this invitation in her hand, that piece of gossip appeared to be every bit as true as the rumors about her.

The ancient springs groaned as she sat down on a corner of her bed. But what did her furnished room matter anymore? This envelope in her hand was an invitation to local society. She'd been waiting a long time for this. She knew somebody would appreciate her, even in a hick burg like this. She knew how to be nice—very nice—to sick old men. She'd show them all what a real woman would do.

From now on, Martine Burden came first. She still had her youth. She was a good-looking woman. She'd make all of them pay.

Maybe she needed to get dressed after all. She finally had a reason to celebrate.

SEVEN

So Stauf took his knife and turned a piece of wood into a doll.

He had whittled some when he was younger, but he had never been very good. He had lacked the patience to practice. Now something else guided his hand. Maybe it was the voices; maybe it was the doll itself. Henry didn't question his new ability; it was enough that he had been given the gift.

When he was finished, the doll matched his earlier vision in every detail. This time, he was careful not to look too closely at the doll's eyes. That gaze was meant for someone else.

Now the doll had been carved, but it wasn't ready. Stauf pulled his shirttails from his pants and ripped off a few inches of fabric to make a rough dress. His coat would cover the tear. His shirt was of no importance compared to the doll.

Then the doll was dressed and his work was done. He looked up, aware of the world around him for the first time in hours. The sun was already low over the lake to the west. Most of the afternoon had passed while he was carving.

His mouth felt dry and empty. He knew only one cure for that. He hadn't tasted alcohol in over a week. And the doll was done. He needed to celebrate. If he had thought about having a drink before, now he lived for it.

He had nothing but his doll, so he took that. The doll would give him strength. Maybe it would even tell him what to do.

Stauf frowned at the alleyway in the fading afternoon light, trying to remember the exact location of the speakeasy. There were no outside markings of any kind. The entrance was one of half a dozen nearly identical doors that lined the narrow lane. Like most establishments of this sort, you only found out about it if you knew the right people. Of course, Henry Stauf knew some of the best drunks around.

In slightly better times he had come by this place with a couple of his drinking buddies. He'd been in here two, maybe three times. His memory wasn't good on that kind of detail. These days, he didn't remember much at all besides what the voices told him.

His feet seemed to remember what his mind forgot. He walked to the third door on the left. The rest of the routine leapt into his mind as he rapped sharply on the door three times and shouted "Delivery!"

The door opened just enough so that somebody on the other side could look him up and down.

He heard muffled voices on the other side of the door. Maybe they were debating whether or not to let him in. He knew he didn't exactly look like he was made of money. It seemed to take forever, waiting for the door to either swing open or slam shut in his face.

Henry Stauf pulled the doll from his pocket and cradled it in both hands, putting it between him and the doorway.

The door swung open. "Come on in," a voice called from inside.

Stauf had known the doll would help him.

He stepped inside. The room was large and dim and filled with a haze of smoke, even though the place was almost empty. The joint had no windows, Stauf realized, no place for air or light to creep in and disturb the drinkers. And no easy way for anything inside to get out again. That was alright with him, too.

There was a sign over the bar, bright yellow letters out-lined in red. "The Come-On Inn." So that was the name of the place. Just like the man said.

There wasn't much business this time of the afternoon. Just a couple of other drunks like him. In half an hour or so, they'd get the laborers after work. The party crowd would take over an hour or two after that, giving up at last to those late-night cops who showed up the minute they were off duty. Cops were some of the biggest spenders around. Who cared about Prohibition when you needed a good stiff drink? And Stauf had drunk with them all, here and in a hundred places just like this.

A chubby, middle-aged guy stood behind the bar. His skin was a pasty white, as if he never left his bar to see the light of day, while his mustache gave his mouth a perpetual frown, the sort of guy who had heard every hard luck story forwards and backwards. Stauf wondered how he was go-ing to ask a guy like that for a drink.

At the moment, though, the barkeep was busy frowning down at the other end of the bar at a girl who was only seven or eight.

"So, where's the bucket?" the barkeep demanded.

"I'm not gonna wash the floor!" the girl replied defiantly, her tiny hands grabbing fistfuls of her worn jumper. She stomped both her feet on the worn wooden floorboards, her pigtails swinging against her cheeks as she vehemently shook her head.

The barman leaned forward over the bar. "You'll do what I—"

"The other girls all went down to the candy store!" the girl added quickly. She stomped both her feet one more time. "I never get to do anything!"

The barkeep took a deep breath. "You'll get something when you've finished—"

"You never give me anything!" The girl's voice rose to a scream. "I hate you!"

The argument grew from there, adult and child screaming at each other, fighting as if no one else was in the room. Looking at the other drunks around the place, a couple of them with their heads on the table, the others staring into space, Stauf guessed that maybe the screamers were the only ones really here after all.

The barman was shouting now, his face the kind of red you saw on rotting vegetables. The girl had given up on words and just stood screaming at the top of her lungs.

Stauf decided this was as good a time as any. He walked up to the bar.

The barkeep shook his head as Stauf approached.

"Mister," he shouted over his daughter's shrieks, "you must want a drink pretty bad to walk over here in the middle of all this." He looked Stauf over quickly, taking in the ragged clothes and unshaved face. "You got something to pay me with?"

Stauf lifted the doll onto the bar. "I've got this."

"What?" The barman's look of confusion turned to one of wonder as he studied Stauf's handiwork. "Quite a piece of carving." The barkeep looked at Henry. "You willing to trade this?"

Stauf nodded. He knew this was what the doll was for. He glanced over at the little girl.

But she was no longer in the far corner of the room. She was walking toward Stauf and his doll, wide-eyed, as if she had never seen anything like what Stauf held in his hand.

"Karen?" the barkeep called softly.

She didn't answer, but only came closer still. Karen stared at the doll, and the doll stared back at her.

Stauf held the doll out to her. "Take it," he said.

Karen looked up at her father for the first time. "Can I?"

The barkeep glanced up at Stauf, then back at his daughter. "I don't see why not, a fine doll like that."

Karen grabbed the doll with a great shriek of delight. Stauf smiled down at the little girl with her new treasure. If anything, he was happier than Karen. He'd done something else for the voices, after all.

But Stauf had other needs as well. He licked his dry lips and looked back to the bartender.

"Can we do a little business here?"

The bartender chuckled at that. "Mister, for giving her that doll, I'll give you drinks all afternoon."

So the barkeep started pouring, and Stauf started drinking. Bourbon, with a beer chaser. The first one burned his throat, but warmed the rest of him. He couldn't remember the last time he felt this good.

"My name's Hans." Stauf looked up to see a hand stuck in front of his face. The barman stood behind it. The mouth behind the mustache broke into a grin.

Stauf took the barman's hand and shook it. "Henry."

"So where'd you get that doll?" Hans asked.

Stauf finished off the bourbon and started on the beer. "Made it. Found a piece of wood about the right size for a doll and carved it in the park."

Karen laughed and sang behind him. He turned around to look at her as he took another drink. She ran around and around in front of the bar, swinging the doll back and forth as if she'd found a dancing partner for life.

The barkeep whistled. "I've never seen her this happy."

Little Karen held the doll close, whispering to it in words that didn't carry to the bar.

Stauf wondered if the doll answered.

"And you made this doll yourself?" Hans asked.

"Just me and my knife," Stauf agreed. "It's a gift I have."

The barkeep scratched at his moustache as he studied his daughter and her new toy. He glanced back at Stauf. "Listen, I got a spare room, back behind the bar. A workshop, too." He nodded at the little girl. "Her mother's dead. It's not much of a life for a little girl, growing up in a bar. Make a couple more toys for my daughter. I'll give you room and board for a week."

Henry Stauf nodded and smiled.

"I need another drink," he pointed out.

This was only the beginning.

EIGHT

Julia Heine stared down into her brandy. It was her sole comfort now. Nobody cared about her anymore, all alone, a retired lady. "Retired." That's what they called what they had done to her, but Julia knew better.

They had been so unfeeling at the bank. She had needed a brandy or two to see her through the long days—a pair at lunch perhaps, and another at coffee time. She really couldn't survive without them. And they had hardly affected her performance at all, at least most of the time. So one day she couldn't add and she got the giggles. You'd think they'd have wanted some fun at the bank, too!

But, no, all they were good at was issuing warnings and ushering her into stern Mr. Frank's office. "This is your last chance," he'd said with such a long frown that Julia had wished she could have another drink, right then and there, just to spite him!

One day, she was ushered into Frank's office and told she no longer worked there. She would be retired, effective immediately. It was better for both the bank's reputation and her own. She was only a few years short of the proper age, anyway.

The proper age? A woman like her became invisible. The bankers could so easily let her go and replace her with someone younger. The moment you slid into middle age and lost your looks . . . poof! You were gone. Just like Julia Heine.

She took another sip of her brandy. It calmed her considerably. A woman just needed a little something to see her through. Especially a woman who was all alone, like Julia.

Or so she'd thought for all these months, until today. That elegant invitation. She had been so surprised, she could even ignore the rudeness of the mailman. "Not another one," he'd muttered as she'd signed for the envelope. Whatever had that meant? How dare that scrawny postman with his thick glasses criticize her private mail. Or was he criticizing her?

She'd been excited just holding the envelope in her hand. Even the quality of the paper spoke of money. You learned to notice things like that, working at a bank.

But she never expected the wonderful prize within: An invitation, a personal invitation, from Henry Stauf.

She remembered how she'd first learned about Stauf, during those long afternoons spent in the Come-On Inn.

Everybody had been so excited that day, talking about the doll Stauf had made for the owner's daughter. Karen, that was her name—the daughter's name, not the doll's. Julia could still remember details like that, no matter what they said down at the bank.

Julia remembered touching Karen's doll. It was remarkable enough to look at, less than a foot long and yet so full of detail that it almost looked alive. But Julia only realized how truly special it was when she held it in her hands. The doll appeared to be made of wood, but the wood was warm, as if it had been carved not from a dead branch but from a living tree, and somehow lived still. The doll was a marvel. Julia couldn't help being interested in the man who could make such a thing.

But why would she, of all people, get a dinner invitation from such a wealthy man? Well, she had always noticed Stauf when he came in to make a deposit. Even with all that money, he had seemed a very frugal person, never bothering to buy new clothes, letting his hair go months between cuts, sometimes going a week or more without a shave. He came and went quickly, as if he even begrudged his time at the bank. He had time for nothing but his toys.

But she had always suspected there was something deeper to Mr. Stauf. Julia would never underestimate others in the way others had underestimated her. Surely, he had seen her at the bank, thought her special enough to single her out for a special evening. An invitation like this was like getting a whole new life.

She could talk to somebody like Stauf, a wealthy older man, the kind of man who could truly appreciate a mature woman. She wondered if he would ask her to call him Henry.

A whole new life. She should send her old life off in style. The brandy was so warming, so reassuring. Another drink or two couldn't hurt.

She thought about Karen as the brandy slid down her throat. The poor girl had died a few months ago, after a sudden, intense illness. And some of those around town had claimed it had something to do with the doll.

Julia Heine thought it was likely, but not exactly in the way the others meant. Poor little Karen had been too young for the great gift she had been given. She just hadn't been strong enough to accept the doll's life-giving energy.

Julia, though, was different. She had the kind of strength that came from too many years of living. She was eager to touch that energy again. She would take that life. She would show them all.

Julia had the desire. She would unlock the secrets of Henry Stauf. Secrets that could take a life, or create one, or start a life all over again, as if it were brand new.

Julia had known this was possible from the moment she held that doll. Maybe Stauf had seen that within her, realized that she was a woman of depth far beyond the "retired lady" everyone else saw.

That would explain this invitation.

Somehow, she would use this dinner party to learn Stauf's secrets. Somehow, she would take the energy that Stauf had put into his creations and use it on herself.

She sighed and sipped at her brandy.

Somehow, Julia Heine would be young again.

NINE

The bar got crowded. And everyone was talking about the doll.

Henry Stauf sipped his beer and took it all in. He knew that his hands, guided by the voices, would fashion other things. People would call them toys, but they would be far more than that.

Looking down at Karen holding her doll, Stauf knew now that he had carved that figure just for her, to fill a hole in her life. Maybe it reminded her of a school friend, an imaginary playmate, even her dead mother. Through the knife in Stauf's hands, the voices had given the little girl what she had wanted most in the world.

Someday, Karen would be asked for something in return. The voices never did anything for free.

The bartender no longer had to buy him drinks. Everybody else wanted to. Every fat-assed citizen of this little stinking burg, all the men and women who didn't have a dime for Stauf the week before, all the good citizens who had looked right through him before he'd made his first gift. Everybody wanted a doll.

And Stauf himself was changing. Maybe it was some silent message from the voices, holding him back. Maybe it was all this new attention from solid townspeople. Whatever the reason, for the first time in years, Stauf no longer wanted to drink himself into oblivion. After the first couple of shots, he started to pace himself. Oh, liquor was still fine, and it helped some. But drinking was no longer enough. Now he had work to do. Now he had a way to pay back everyone for all they'd done to him.

Everyone asked what else he would carve. He told them all to wait and see. He had no more an idea than they did what the voices and his hands would produce next. All he knew was that when he made it, someone would need it—very, very much.

"I have to make a few things for Hans here," Stauf explained to the others, waving generously at the busy barkeep behind him. "But, after a week or so I might have some free time on my schedule. Come see me then."

A few of the more insistent patrons tried to place orders, but he shook his head and turned them away, finally ready for some serious drinking.

"Next week!" the rich bastards called.

"See you then!" They smiled at him as if he were their friend.

"We're counting on you!" The pushiest among them waved like they were glad to have him on the team.

Stauf was counting on them, too. He downed another shot. It appeared that he had a lifetime full of work—for both himself and the voices.

Late that night, Henry Stauf made his second toy. At least that's what all the people in the town would call it.

This one was a puzzle, carved from new pieces of wood, then painted and screwed and glued together to form a single large board—a board with thirty-two squares, red and black, which had to be arranged in a checkerboard pattern, with no two reds or blacks directly touching.

It looked like simplicity itself. But there was only one way to solve it. The voices made sure of that.

They had also told him how to make the colors to paint the squares, colors that came from certain plants and the blood of dead animals. The colors made the puzzle come alive. It was just like the doll; you could stare at that design for hours.

The voices had given him something more. He had been able to look beyond the puzzle. He had seen shapes there; how many he wasn't sure. They were only vague forms, lost in the haze beyond the glowing puzzle.

How he longed to see the faces behind the voices!

But it was too soon for that. He had a great deal of work to do. Perhaps the voices would let him see them someday, when he was worthy.

Stauf woke then and went to find the things he needed. They were all—wood and weeds and a dying dog on the road—exactly where the voices said they would be. Then he returned to the workshop behind the bar and began.

He remembered, as he worked, how good the hammer had felt in his hand, that day in the park. It occurred to him then that the doll he had made, and the puzzle he was making now, were much the same as that hammer. All three were instruments of power, given to him by the voices.

By leading him to the hammer, the voices had given him control over life and death. These toys, his new tools, were instruments of control as well, subtler than the hammer. In a flash, he saw the doll he had made, the puzzle he was working on, and hundreds of other toys he had yet to shape. Somehow, for one instant, all of them looked like little hammers.

Henry Stauf blinked. He was going to use those hammers to strike out at this whole fat-ass town.

So he returned to work. And as he worked, the voices seemed to come closer. They caressed him with their whispers and comforted him when he was deep in dreams.

Every time he made another doll, another puzzle, he came that much closer to seeing it all.

Stauf's success grew with every passing day.

Even the best children could be difficult sometimes. Oh, you could talk to them, reason with them, even discipline them. But while that took care of the immediate problem, there was always bound to be another difficulty just down the line.

Ah, but the children who had gotten Stauf's toys never seemed to complain. Hans' daughter smiled all the time now, the doll clutched close to her chest, lost in her own little world. The other youngsters who received Stauf's handiwork, whether a stern toy soldier or another very compelling puzzle, acted much the same. The toy was their life.

Everyone wants to make their children happy and well-behaved. Rather than talking, cajoling, or spanking, how much easier to give them a wonderful toy?

The parents fought for Stauf's creations. He could name almost any price for his latest marvel. Money flowed to him. At first, only the richest in town could afford his services. But that was fine with Stauf. Fat cats first, after all.

In only a couple of months, he opened his very own Toy Shop. The real estate brokers found him a prime storefront, the banker arranged a generous loan, all in exchange for his special toys. The local newspaper editor ran free ads and even came up with a slogan for the toymaker's new enterprise, "A Stauf Toy Is a Toy for Life."

Stauf would make very special toys for each of them in turn. Toys that could take over their children's lives, just like the slogan said.

And on a chilly winter's day, Stauf's Toy Shop opened for the rest of town.

Not all the toys were his. Henry Stauf carried a few games and toys from the outside world. He could only work so fast on his own creations, after all, and he needed something to fill the shelves. Besides, he could always look over the other toys and steal a good idea here and there, twist it a bit and give it that personal touch.

Of course, the toys that sold the best were the ones he made. Most sold within hours, and all within days, of Henry placing them on the shelves. Parents bought them eagerly, to fill the holes in their children's lives. Sometimes the parents were desperate, as if they were filling holes in their lives as well.

Stauf rarely slept, and he turned down all invitations that would take him out of the shop. He had to make new toys constantly to keep up with the demand. Somehow, he managed to create three or four new ones every single day. The voices showed him the way, and they gave him strength.

It was almost as if the owners of the voices were working by his side in the back room of his shop. They seemed to be waiting for him at the edge of sight, as if he might catch a glimpse of one at any moment from the corners of his eyes. Not that he ever did, really. But he knew he would see them soon.

And when he saw them, the voices would give him his reward.

TEN

Magic was his life.

Hamilton Temple had headlined once. The 1902 World's Fair, part of Billy Rose's island of side shows. "THE MAGNIFICENT DR. TEMPLE PERFORMS FEATS OF MAGIC AND MYSTERY!" the banner had proclaimed. "SEE WONDERS FROM EVERY CORNER OF THE GLOBE!" And from high noon until the small hours of morning, people would stand in line to see those feats of wonder, great lines snaking out of the tent. People who wanted to believe.

He had been one of the greats, making cards and doves and flowers appear from nowhere, cutting and reassembling beautiful women with a wave of a wand. He had performed a thousand different illusions, with tours of Europe and South America, crossing the continental United States more than twenty times, his name prominently mentioned on the vaudeville bills of over a hundred theaters from Bangor, Maine, to San Diego, California.

But vaudeville wasn't what it used to be, and neither was Hamilton Temple. They were saying that these new talking pictures would kill off vaudeville for good. Not that this made much difference to Temple. His fingers had grown too old, too crippled with arthritis. There was no more magic left in them. Everything had slipped away.

No, Temple reminded himself, not everything. His fingers failed him, yet his mind was still sharp.

When you specialize in illusions, you have to carefully observe what is real. And Temple had observed much these past few months.

He had seen the changes that had come to their town. And he knew that, in some way, Henry Stauf was behind them all.

He looked back at the card and the very personal letter on the dressing table. He was not at all surprised that Stauf was as aware of him as Temple was of Stauf. In a way, they were brothers, both dabbling in those realms just beyond the real. In fact, he had been expecting something like this invitation for some time—ever since Henry Stauf disappeared, really.

He had seen Stauf graduate from common craftsman to the richest man in town. And he had done it all with those strange toys—toys filled with power. Somehow, Stauf was the conduit for that power, the gateway between this world and—somewhere else. Temple could think of no other explanation. This was no ordinary magic. While Temple suspected these things existed, Stauf lived them.

The more Temple learned about Stauf, the more excited he became. A power like this went beyond human frailty. No mere parlor tricks here. This magic could cause a man to be reborn.

Living a life largely on the road, and a life steeped in illusion, Hamilton Temple didn't believe in much. But he did believe in Henry Stauf.

He grabbed his coat and hat and strode through the door. The guests were to gather at the Stauf house at 7 p.m. It was almost the appointed time.

This was one appointment he didn't want to be late for. Whatever happened tonight, Hamilton Temple knew this was his last chance.

ELEVEN

Such a shame," the townspeople whispered.

Stauf frowned from the back of his shop, where he was putting the finishing touches on a toy gun, a miniature replica of the revolver he'd thrown away. All that had happened only a few months ago, but it felt like another lifetime.

Three well-dressed women were clustered at the far side of the shop, talking in the sort of voices that carried only half their words to Stauf's ears.

"—so suddenly—" one murmured.

"—taking it so badly—" another agreed.

"—his only daughter—" the first one continued.

"—and after the way his wife—" the third added in tones of equal concern.

These days, Stauf tried to keep out of the everyday operation of the store. He'd hired a young lady to take care of most of the business. She smiled and greeted the customers so he didn't have to. She was a pretty little thing, really, and got on well with children. And she wore those shameless short skirts the young favored so much. Once, Stauf would have wanted to do more with her than simply let her run his shop.

Now, though, he only had time for the toys.

"Such a shame—"

"—So quickly—"

"The baker's son has the same—"

The girl was hovering close to the chattering women. Stauf was getting another of his feelings, that this gossip was something he should hear.

He waved for the shopgirl to come over to his workbench.

She frowned back at him, pausing a moment before she approached him, as if she was a little afraid of him. That was fine with Stauf. The more people who were afraid of him, the better.

"Is there something wrong?" he asked quietly when she was by the bench at last.

"It's terrible, sir," she answered. "The bartender's daughter, little Karen, she's dead."

"Dead?" he said back, repressing an urge to smile. He'd been expecting something like this for quite some time.

"The women said it happened very quickly," the shopgirl continued. "They say she clutched her Stauf toy to the end."

Stauf nodded. That, too, was only to be expected.

"Other children are sick, too. It really is very upsetting."

"Do you think all the sick children have Stauf toys?" he asked.

She looked at him strangely. "What an odd question to ask, sir. But I imagine just about every child in town has at least one of your toys."

Stauf nodded one more time, then returned to his work.

This was what the voices had wanted, after all.

Children died, a lot of children, maybe one of every three little boys and girls in town. But what did that matter, when it let Stauf come closer to the truth?

He knew now that every toy was a transaction. He made them to complete people's lives. And once those people

were given something, they had to give something in return. The voices demanded that.

The young and the weak often paid with their lives. The
voices were hungry. And the more the voices gave Stauf to
produce, the more the voices required.

They needed more, and they were always closer. Every
transaction brought them nearer to Stauf's shop, so close
that sometimes he felt he might be brushing by them in
the dark.

The voices were so close now that the little toy shop was
beginning to feel crowded. The shopgirl had run away one
afternoon and refused to return, saying that she, too, was
ill. When Stauf talked to her on the phone, all he could hear
was fear.

Stauf realized this little place was no longer enough. He
needed a better place for his toys. He needed to build a
house The voices wanted that. The voices needed that. The
house would give the voices a place to stay, a place to join
Stauf in this world.

But in a way, the house would be the biggest toy of all.
Stauf knew now that all his puzzles, all his toys, contained
both life and death. Stauf would fill his new house with
puzzles, too. But in these newest puzzles, death would be
a little closer.

The voices cried out to Stauf, imploring him in his
dreams, whispering at him from the shop's dark corners,
shouting at him in every pound of a hammer or swish of a
saw. Although the voices held no words as Stauf remembered them, he still knew what they were saying.

Give us the house, they called. *Give it to us and we will
give to you.*

And Stauf would do what they said. For he knew, whatever the voices wanted, the house would protect him, even
as he prepared the way.

Stauf knew this part of his work was ending.

The children were dying, and the poor townspeople were tormented by the horror of so many funerals; so many small caskets.

Still, in a much larger way, it was only the beginning.

Work soon began in earnest on the Stauf mansion. Money was no object, and teams of contractors used Stauf's own strange sketches to realize his bizarre vision. No team ever saw the full plan. No one ever understood that this wasn't just another house, or suspected that the sum of its parts would frame an almost limitless potential for evil.

The work went quickly, hastened by the hordes of builders laboring day and night, supported by Stauf's seemingly endless supply of funds, and perhaps, in a way only suspected by Stauf himself, spurred along by an accident that claimed one worker's life. A man fell from the pinnacle of the house to the cold earth and an instant death below.

Such things happen, the foreman told Stauf apologetically.

Yes. Stauf nodded in sad agreement. Such things happen all the time.

As the house neared completion, Stauf closed his toy shop. It had only been open at odd times lately. People didn't think about toys anymore; not when some terrible disease was claiming their children.

Experts came from New York to try to diagnose the illness and stop the horrible deaths. The local paper reported how they examined the dead and the dying, how they took samples of blood and urine, how they were studying the problem.

But that's all they could do. Stauf knew they would find no answers. At least none that they would understand.

When the house was completed and Stauf had paid the last of the workmen, a simple announcement appeared in the newspaper:

Stauf's Toy Shop Closes its Doors Forever.

And Stauf disappeared.

Some people imagined that he had left town for good to travel the world. Perhaps, many others theorized, he was a recluse in his mansion, distraught over so many children dying. A man like Stauf must have loved children.

Or, perhaps, he had simply made enough money, and shut himself away from the world.

Of course, no one could guess the truth. Even Stauf himself didn't know exactly what he was waiting for.

But Stauf did know that the voices wouldn't make him wait for long. He would have his reward at last, once the voices told him what they really wanted.

TWELVE

He looks up at the house, the house where people die. After all, he's heard the rumors.

A small town lives on rumors. In this town, most of the rumors have to do with Henry Stauf. The house that Henry Stauf built sits alone now, atop the town's highest hill. It is a large place, the sort of place worthy of being called a mansion if it were only in better repair. Bricks have tumbled from the chimney; wood buckles along the porch railings. Even part of the hillside has crumbled away, leaving the house sitting atop a sheer precipice.

Sometimes, people passing by the old Stauf place swear they can see lights in the upper windows, although maybe they are only seeing reflections of the moon. Sometimes, people who live nearby swear there are noises, but maybe they only hear the wind, or some nocturnal creature's cry from the mansion's overgrown yard.

Sometimes, though, the noises sound like screams.

He looks up at the house, and realizes vaguely that he has stood here many times before, wondering about this place, about Stauf, about his toys.

He wonders about the children who died, and feels for an instant that it had something to do with Stauf and his puzzles.

But mostly he wonders—has the mansion always looked this way? Certainly, though perhaps an eternity ago, the bricks were bright red, the wood polished, the paint glistening. Yet somehow the slow process of rotting seems to be the structure's natural state.

Has Stauf been hiding in the house for years, a disturbed old hermit? Or is it only days since Stauf shut his toy store and walked away from his puzzles?

But maybe this house is another puzzle, too.

How long has it been since the children died? How long since Stauf disappeared? God, how long has he been looking at this house, standing outside the decayed mansion, thinking about the sick children's rhymes about Stauf, thinking, remembering something that happened long ago—

Or maybe something that hasn't happened yet.

The children who are still alive are drawn to the place. They gather outside the mansion's wrought iron gates day after day, as if they know something no one else will speak of; as if they know every rumor is true.

He listens, and he can hear them sing:

> "Old Man Stauf built a house,
> And filled it with his toys.
> Seven guests all came one night;
> Their screams the only noise."

Seven guests. Seven invitations.

> "Blood inside the library,
> Blood right down the hall,
> Blood going up the attic stairs
> Where the last guest did fall."

It is the children's song. He knows the words so well he could sing along.

> "Not one soul came out that night.
> No one was ever seen.
> But Old Mad Stauf is waiting there,
> Crazy, sick and mean . . ."

He knows the song by heart. But how?
He almost remembers.

THIRTEEN

Martine Burden led the way, and the others followed. Six people climbed the steep pathway and steps to gather at the great oak door with the inlaid, stained glass window.

Martine was surprised by how weathered the boards looked on the front of the house. The pillars on either side of the front door looked like they could use a new coat of paint as well. The rest of the place wasn't that well kept, either, with leaves littering the porch and bird-droppings crusted on the iron handrail by the stairs. Wasn't this house almost brand new? She wondered if Stauf had skimped on labor or used the cheapest paint. In her experience, it was the sort of thing people with money did—pinch pennies everywhere. That, she supposed, was why they still had money. But still, Stauf's graying mansion looked almost more like a derelict hovel than one of the proudest dwellings in town.

Martine stepped forward and pulled a rope-cord that hung by the side of the door. Like everything around it, the blue cord looked like it had once been quite elegant, but now appeared a little the worse for wear. Still, frayed or not, it should ring a bell somewhere inside. She listened as she pulled down harder a second time, but no sound came back to her from within the house.

The front door remained closed.

"Perhaps we weren't meant to come here after all," someone said behind her. Martine turned to see Elinor Knox cowering against her husband. What could she be so frightened of?

"Perhaps someone should knock," Julia Heine said dryly from where she stood by the Knoxes' side.

"Here," volunteered the youngest of the three male guests. He stepped by Martine before she could turn back to the door. "Let me try."

This was Brian Dutton, the thirtyish businessman. All six of them had introduced themselves as they climbed the path, but Martine still had to think a minute to keep the names straight.

Dutton knocked firmly on the wooden portion of the large door, as Martine allowed herself to study the large stained glass window that took up most of the door's upper half. It was difficult to make out any details of the window's design, since no light shone from the house's interior.

No one to answer the door, no welcoming light. Perhaps Elinor Knox was right, and they weren't supposed to be here after all. Maybe this was all someone's idea of an elaborate practical joke. Maybe Henry Stauf really was dead, just like the gossips said.

"One thing I've learned in business is to be persistent," Dutton announced, knocking even more forcefully. He smiled at Martine. He was an attractive man in his way, although there was something about the fussy manner in which he dressed, and the walking stick he carried, that put Martine off.

No. She knew exactly what it was. It was Dutton's attitude, the arrogant way he looked down at the others, his

I'm privileged and I can do anything way of walking up and banging on the door. She had seen that attitude before, in fact had once found it very attractive.

Brian Dutton reminded her very much of Siegfried. She had been left once by a man like that. She wouldn't make the same mistake twice.

Still, no one came to the door.

Apparently, Stauf meant to keep them waiting.

"Here," Hamilton Temple said from the back of the group. "I've had some experience with trick locks and the like. Let me try."

Trick locks? Martine suppressed a laugh. Just what was Mr. Temple expecting to find in this place?

Martine wondered what Stauf would want with an eccentric old man like Temple, anyway. She knew he had been a stage magician once, a long time ago. He was dressed like one tonight. What exactly was he trying to prove with that cape and turban?

Temple pushed his way past the others and pressed on a panel at the door's center. The door swung open at his touch.

Martine was a little impressed, despite herself. Mr. Temple might be a very good man to have around. Too bad he was so old.

Stepping inside, Martine half expected to see a doorman, perhaps a servant who had been instructed to wait until he was sure all the guests had arrived before he opened the door.

But the front hall was empty. Worse, it wasn't very clean. Everything, furniture, rugs, paintings, even the light fixtures, all seemed coated with a fine layer of dust. Spiderweb strands glistened in the dim light given off by dust-covered bulbs. Not that the light reached everywhere. Much of the place was in shadow.

Henry Stauf apparently didn't believe in cleaning for company.

She stepped forward, looking down at an ornate brocade sofa pushed against the wall. The sofa's covering looked frayed, with odd, uneven lumps beneath the fabric, as if the springs were broken underneath.

"My," she said sarcastically, "isn't this a cheery place?"

She stepped out of the way as the Knoxes followed. Elinor Knox literally clung to her husband's side, her hands grabbing his suit coat. Edward Knox, for his part, seemed pleased as punch to serve as his wife's protector. Sometimes, Martine wished she could depend on someone like that.

Elinor Knox looked timidly out from her husband's shadow. "Eddie," she said softly, "I don't know if we should have come."

Edward Knox reminded Martine of nothing so much as a rooster protecting a henhouse. "Why?" he demanded. "Just because it's a spooky old house? Don't worry. I'm here to watch out for you."

"What a dump!" Julia Heine exclaimed as she walked through the doorway. "I expected more from Mr. Stauf." Martine wondered why it was so important for this aging woman to put on this sort of act. From the looks of her somewhat worn attire, Julia Heine hadn't seen the finer things in quite some time.

Brian Dutton wrinkled his nose as he leaned on his walking stick. "And, God—it smells awful, too. What's Stauf been doing here?"

The minute Dutton mentioned it, Martine noticed the smell. There was a faint odor to this place, a sense of decay as pervasive as the dust.

Martine didn't care what Stauf did with his money. In fact, the less he spent on this place, the more he would have to give to her! She glanced at the others around her. Despite all the criticism of their surroundings, everyone was trying to smile, ready to have a good time. She guessed that no one else was eager to leave, at least until Henry Stauf had given them whatever he had promised.

Hamilton Temple glanced back at the stained glass window as the door slammed shut behind him.

"It's a puzzle!"

It took her a moment to realize that Temple was talking about the stained glass window itself, an intricate design that Martine couldn't quite make sense of. So Stauf put his toys and puzzles in his house as well. Martine imagined this whole place would be full of surprises.

After all, the door had shut without any help from Mr. Temple.

Brian Dutton walked down the hallway, trying doors. The first one was locked. First, they couldn't get into the house. Now would all the other doors be locked, trapping them in the hallway? This was a damned peculiar way to treat invited guests.

But the next door opened easily. Beyond was a well-appointed dining room, complete with a dark cherry table fully set for dinner. Maybe, Dutton thought, they were expected after all.

There were seven plates, with seven envelopes. Each envelope bore a set of initials—H.T., M.B., J.H.—written in a slightly cramped script, the same script he had seen on his own invitation. Dutton wondered if this was Stauf's handwriting; he would have thought someone who made such wonderful toys would have a showier penmanship.

Seven envelopes for six guests; did the last envelope belong to Stauf himself? Dutton walked along the far side of the table, glancing at the envelopes as he passed: E.K., Mrs. E.K., and B.D.

This was for him, then. The seventh envelope sat on the place setting at the head of the table. But that envelope had no initials at all. It was totally blank.

He looked up as he heard others come into the room. Elinor and Edward Knox looked down at the envelopes on the plates. Elinor snatched up the one addressed to her.

"I guess the party's beginning," Dutton quipped.

Knox nodded, glancing quickly about the room. He looked no happier than Dutton felt.

But why delay the inevitable? He picked up the envelope with his initials on it. He stepped back out into the hallway to give himself a bit of privacy, then pulled out the paper inside and quickly unfolded it. It appeared to be some sort of personal note from Stauf.

As he read, he could almost hear old man Stauf speaking the words, the raspy voice of the toymaker echoing almost as if they both stood in Stauf's dusty shop.

"My dear Mr. Dutton. Welcome to my house. The arrangement is simple. You are to spend the night as my guest. And, in exchange, I will give you your heart's most secret desire.

"And you know what that is, Mr. Dutton, don't you? But I require one thing of you—a special service, a task that I've set up especially for you."

How could Stauf know anything about Dutton? The two of them had never met. But this "service" he mentioned—Stauf must have had a special reason for inviting Dutton. And he must have somehow known Dutton would come.

Well, why not? Henry Stauf was a very rich man. And rich men could have eyes and ears everywhere, especially in a small town like this, where everybody knew at least some of everybody else's business. Stauf could know quite a bit about Brian Dutton, like the fact that he was a businessman, and what kind of businessman he was. Maybe Stauf even knew how Dutton had gotten to be a survivor.

Dutton frowned at the letter. He wished the playing field were a little more even here. He'd feel a lot better if he knew a bit more about Henry Stauf.

His thoughts were disturbed by Julia Heine's laughter. She seemed to find something very funny. Dutton wondered for an instant what worth Stauf might find in an aging hypocrite like her. The socialite, that overbearing Knox and his mousy wife, the retired magician; why had the toymaker chosen such an odd assortment of guests?

He could hear the other guests talking in the room he had just left. One of the women, he thought it was Mrs. Knox, made a general remark about how nice it was for Stauf to invite them all. Martine snapped back that, if this was an invitation, where was their host? Edward Knox huffed something about Stauf having his reasons, which started Julia Heine laughing all over again.

They talked on like that for another few moments, small talk, mostly, not saying much of value, as if all the guests feared that, if they gave away something too personal, it would give one of the other guests—one of their competitors—an extra chance to win.

In a way, Dutton realized, even though they were all here together, they were all here by themselves. That was Stauf's doing, too. But why?

If there were any answers, they might be hidden in the letter. He read on:

"One guest hasn't arrived yet, a guest unlike the six of you. A very special guest. Your service involves that guest. You may wonder what that service is. But that is the game, Mr. Dutton. The puzzle I've set before you.

"This is all I will tell you, Mr. Dutton. In the morning, only one of the guests will walk out of the house, with his or her every wish granted."

The letter was signed "Your host, Henry Stauf."

So there might be a mysterious guest and some even more mysterious service he had to perform? There were no answers here, only more crazy questions. Exactly what kind of game was this Stauf playing?

Julia's laughter echoed behind him.

Dutton looked back into the dining room. The others had all gathered there now. He guessed it would be best if he joined them.

He walked back into the dining room. "I guess our host wants us to fend for ourselves."

Julia had gotten into the wine. That alone might be reason enough for her laughter.

She drained her glass and made a face. "I've tasted better."

Often, Dutton imagined.

Temple held up his envelope. "At least he left his regrets—"

Martine Burden waved her envelope under Edward Knox's nose.

"I'll show you mine, if you'll show me yours."

Edward Knox looked back to the socialite, beads of sweat appearing on his brow. He stole a glance at his wife as he answered.

"I—I—I don't know."

Elinor was staring at a cake on the table, a cake Dutton hadn't seen before. How had it gotten there? Maybe one of the others had carried it from the kitchen. Or maybe Henry Stauf was moving around behind the scenes, carrying cakes and other things when no one was looking. No, Dutton thought, there had to be another explanation. It was just this crazy note in his hand; it gave Dutton the creeps.

Elinor picked up a note placed next to the cake.

"It says we're supposed to each get a piece—exactly the same, with the same symbols."

So this must be the first of the puzzles Stauf had mentioned in his note. The cake was covered with tiny skulls and tiny gravestones—Stauf's idea of a joke, no doubt—seemingly spread at random. So this was one of the puzzles? And they had to solve it. Why? To get "his heart's most secret desire," as Stauf had put it. Dutton wasn't quite sure what that desire would be. Unless it was money. That was something Dutton could always use to get out of that business rat race for good.

A man like Stauf could have hidden millions. And they had to play along with this crazy millionaire until he decided to show up himself, or reveal his prize.

For those kind of stakes, Dutton was willing to play along, at least for now. It looked like the others were willing to do the same.

"Each piece the same?" Julia Heine frowned at the way the symbols were scattered across the cake. "That's impossible."

Dutton didn't agree. There seemed to be some sort of crazy order to the symbols. No, not impossible. Just very, very difficult.

Hamilton Temple picked up a knife. "I believe I have it."

Slowly, methodically, he cut six pieces in such a way that they all contained the same symbols, placing each odd shaped piece in turn on another of the plates.

But what did this puzzle mean? And what would Stauf give them in return?

If this was any indication of the games Stauf was playing, it was going to be a very long night.

FOURTEEN

Elinor had had enough of this puzzle, and all the happy chatter. None of the people in the other room wanted to share anything with each other, really; they would just as soon all the others went away. She was so glad she was here with Edward. They had been a couple for so long, they would never need to be alone.

But, even with Edward there, Elinor needed a little quiet and a place to think. She stepped into the kitchen for a moment alone.

She'd had a bad feeling about this party from the first. She could sense things sometimes, like that time Aunt Bertha had her accident, or the day the neighbors came into that unexpected inheritance. She'd had feelings about both of those before they had happened—what her husband called "her spells." She knew Eddie didn't understand them and sometimes barely tolerated them, thinking them some "female problem." But she knew enough to respect them. And her feelings had never been so on edge as they were this very minute.

What did it mean? All she knew was that something very bad would happen very soon.

She realized she still held the envelope in her hand, the one addressed with her initials. Perhaps she would get some clue to the mystery if she read the note:

"When all seven guests have gathered, you must figure out what I want. It's a puzzle, Mrs. Knox.

"And mind you, the others will be working at the same task. It may all depend on who has the greatest need. Or who is the bravest.

"There are clues throughout this house as to what must be done. You might say that the house is alive with clues.

"Hoping to meet you—in the flesh—I remain,

"Your host, Henry Stauf."

"The house was alive with clues." Is that what she was feeling? The note seemed as crazy as the rest of the house. If her Eddie hadn't wanted to come here so desperately, she would never have set foot in such a place.

But she had seen a change in Eddie on the same day he'd gotten the invitation, a change that she suspected had very little to do with this party. Perhaps it was another bad debt. Although her husband seldom spoke about it, she knew he wasn't very good with money. And he indulged her so!

She really should tell him not to buy her such extravagant things. She had let him pamper her for so many years without a thought as to where all the niceties came from. In her way, she realized, she was as much to blame for their finances as he was. She always meant to sit down with her Eddie and have a long talk about what they had and what they wanted for their future, but somehow, she never did.

Whatever the reason, Eddie had been as upset as she had ever seen him. He had been so desperate to come here—as though Stauf's party might be a matter of life and death—that she couldn't help coming along.

Now, she thought she should have trusted her first feelings about this place. This note in her hand did nothing to calm her; she felt even more than before that something very bad was very close. She would have to watch her "spells," and her surroundings, to make sure the bad things didn't happen to Eddie and herself.

She heard a noise behind her.

There was a door, down a short flight of steps. It must lead down to the basement.

Someone was knocking.

Maybe, she thought, this was one of the clues Henry Stauf had mentioned.

Maybe this was the missing guest. Perhaps, once they were all together, they could get on with this little party, and once it was over Eddie and she could get back to their normal lives.

She walked down the steps to the basement door and turned the knob.

Edward Knox turned away from Martine for an instant to look about the dining room. They were alone for the moment; the others had all left to wander about the house.

He had other things to do, too. He had to find Henry Stauf as quickly as possible and convince the man to lend him money. Surely, when the toymaker saw how desperate he was, Knox could get him to see reason!

Failure to secure funds would lose him his hands, his job, maybe even Elinor. He had to find the money. Nothing else was important.

Well, perhaps in another minute.

He sighed and turned back to the woman. Right now, he didn't want to look anywhere else.

Martine Burden was eyeing him over her now-empty glass of wine. It was a little unnerving to receive this much attention from an attractive younger woman; and he had to admit, with her long, dark hair and that red dress cut low at the shoulders and tight at the waist to flatter her very slim form, she was quite attractive. He did his best not to look at her milky white skin, or the way the dress showed the lines of her breasts. His gaze drifted up to her eyes. She stared straight back at him.

She took a step towards him. He frowned and took a step away.

"Don't worry," she said with the slightest of smiles. "I won't bite."

He looked about quickly, sure that Elinor would be just behind him. But she was nowhere to be seen. It was so unlike her to wander off like that. She couldn't have gone far. He should go look for her. He glanced down at the few drops of wine still in his own glass. Well, perhaps he would do a bit of looking in a minute.

Martine took another step forward. This time, Knox didn't budge. Martine's smile spread across her face.

"Edward," she said softly. "We could help each other. I could help you—and you could help me."

Knox didn't know what to say. Aside from his money problems, his life had become solid, dependable, regular. And it no longer included young women speaking to him like this.

Martine was quite close to him now. Her perfume filled his head.

He smiled at her. He wanted to reach out and touch her cheek, caress her shoulder. He wanted to do things he hadn't done in a very long time.

But what about Elinor? He had been with his wife for such a long time. She trusted him, depended upon him.

But how long had it been since he had seen a woman as young, as beautiful, as *alive* as Martine?

"Come and talk to me in one of the upstairs bedrooms," Martine said, as if she read his mind. "It will be nice and private."

She turned from him then and walked from the room. Knox followed her with his gaze, strangely surprised and predictably delighted at how Martine's dress clung to her curves as she moved.

Perhaps Elinor could take care of herself for a bit.

Perhaps there were other things in life beyond money.

Tonight held possibilities he had never even dreamed of.

Hamilton Temple knew this house held secrets. It would be in keeping with Stauf's fascination with puzzles and games. He was expecting trap doors, hidden compartments, secret passageways—the sort of thing he'd used over and over as a stage magician. That would be perfectly in keeping with a place like this, with its locked doors and too-narrow corridors.

He found a door that opened into a music room, dominated by a grand piano in the center of the room before the windows; a piano which in turn was surrounded by lush green plants. The plants looked rather exotic; they certainly came from somewhere far away from Upstate New York. But then, plants had never been one of Temple's fields of expertise.

Sheet music was propped open on the piano. He would have to come back here and take a closer look, perhaps even attempt to play the tune laid out before him. Stauf had mentioned "looking for clues" in his note to Temple, and anything in this house, from sheet music to plant soil, could be significant.

But for now, Temple wanted to explore as much of this strange mansion, and learn as much about Stauf, as quickly as he could.

He opened another door, which led to a library. Temple knew he could learn a great deal about anyone from the sort of books they read.

Inside, floor to ceiling shelves were crammed with books, save for a space carved for that doorway through which he had just passed, and two more spaces on other walls, one filled with a rather impressive fireplace, the other with a set of glass doors that appeared to lead outside.

It seemed an impressive collection, with a number of books that might interest Temple. He reached for *The Elements of Magic*, a most promising title.

But it wasn't a book at all. The whole wall was hard and wooden, the wood carved and painted to look like book spines.

"Trompe l'oeil," he murmured to himself. It was all a false front, a glorious facade. But a facade implied something beneath. What was this false front hiding?

He ran his hands along the row of false books, until he felt movement beneath his fingers. He stopped, and realized there was a real book here, slid in among these false surfaces.

He pulled the book free of its niche in the wall. *The Tactics of Chess* by Bertram Von Hochenberg. He opened it and saw explanations of chess notation, then a chapter on opening moves.

Opening moves. How much like Stauf, the master of puzzles and games.

Temple heard a noise from beyond the glass doors, outside the house. Still holding the book, he walked to the doors to take a look. There was no moon tonight. The clouds were thick overhead, turning a dark night darker still.

But he thought he saw something moving in the dimness.

He had expected these doors to open on some sort of patio, even a garden, with statues and a fountain. The kind of things you usually saw in these formal gardens, like a frolicking Pan, or those ever-present cherubs holding a cornucopia.

A chuckle formed deep in his throat, but it never made it through his lips.

The mist, the swirling mist, was taking shape in the darkness.

Temple took a step away. The book fell from his fingers. It made a hollow sound as it hit the wooden floor.

The shape in the mist was coming closer. It seemed to press against the glass. It oozed across the window panes like some sort of giant snail, or maybe a slug, coating the glass with a trail of slime.

Temple backed into a chair. He lost his balance and sat abruptly.

The thing on the other side of the window made a sucking sound, as if it were hungry and sensed food on the other side of that too-thin glass.

Temple heard a moan. It took him a moment to realize the sound came from his own throat.

The doors groaned as the thing pressed against them, but, for the moment, they held.

Temple shuddered, and tried to look anywhere but at those doors. Whatever that thing was, there would be no getting out of this house through the garden.

Not while it was still dark.

Elinor opened the door. There was nobody there.

"Hello?" she called tentatively.

She thought she heard an answering voice. But the sound was faint, as if it came from deep in the basement.

Had someone run away when she opened the door? This whole house was a creepy place; she could easily see someone else being as scared as her. The stairs were well lit, though.

"Hello!" she called. "I won't hurt you!"

She took a few steps down, listening for a response. She thought she heard a cry, high and frightened, like that of a child.

She had seen the children playing outside before. Had one wandered inside? The least she could do was go to the bottom of the stairs and take a look.

The old boards creaked beneath her as she took the steps slowly.

"Hello?" she called again. But the response seemed as distant as before.

When she got to the bottom of the stairs, she was surprised to see—not the normal clutter of a basement—but a long, narrow passageway with a single lightbulb at the other end.

A central hallway, she thought, with rooms to either side. It wouldn't hurt to walk a little way down. She wondered if Mr. Stauf was hiding down here. She knew Eddie would not leave until they met him. Maybe, if she found him, they could end their little game and get home at a decent hour.

She came to the end of the corridor, a "T" turning left and right. These must lead to some other rooms, she thought. The wine cellar, perhaps. Or a workshop; toymaker Stauf surely had one of those.

Or a family crypt.

She tried to smile at her foolishness. It was gloomy enough down here for that sort of fantasy. She had almost forgotten about her feelings of dread when she had heard the child cry. Now, in a moment of silence, they threatened to rush back and overwhelm her.

Perhaps she should go back and get some of the others. They could explore this basement together. That certainly sounded much safer.

She heard a shuffling sound to her left. Was it a child, lost in the maze of corridors?

"Hello?" she called again, moving towards the noise, almost despite herself. The sounds seemed so close. This should only take a minute.

The corridor took another left and ended in a wall.

There was no sign of anyone, or anything, that could have made those sounds.

But there was something very bad here. Those feelings were coming back to her. She decided to get some help, and turned to retrace her steps.

Then she heard the shuffling again, this time in front of her. How was that possible? Maybe it was a maze down here, another one of those puzzles Stauf seemed so proud of. She might have gotten a little turned around. She would have to be careful to find her way back.

She really had no idea what was making that noise. Maybe it wasn't a child at all.

Her hand brushed the wall as she turned. It was wet. She rubbed her fingers together. Whatever came from the damp walls was sticky, too. She walked down the corridor toward the single naked lightbulb to get a better look.

The stuff on her hands was brownish-red. Brownish-red like blood.

No! She felt the panic rise up inside her. She had to get out of this place. She started to run, back towards the stairs. The shuffling steps were still ahead of her, but she didn't care. She had to get out of this basement.

She took a right, and then another right. Shouldn't the long corridor leading to the stairs be just ahead? Where had she made a wrong turn?

Something fell onto her face and hands. Blood-red splatters.

"No!" she screamed. But her voice seemed to be swallowed up by the never-ending corridors.

Where could she go? Where could she turn?

She fell to her knees. And felt something behind her, brushing against her ankle.

Something cold and dead.

FIFTEEN

It had been a dare.

And a dare couldn't be ignored.

One of the other kids had said that nobody would have the guts to actually go into the house. Not just to step in the front door, either. To really walk around and see the whole place.

The upstairs. The attic. The cellar.

Nobody would dare.

"I could," Tad had said.

It was all B.S., really, the kind of stuff kids knocked each other about. He looked up as the sun slid behind the hills and the grass in front of the house darkened and lost its color.

From this angle, the house looked like nothing so much as a great black shadow.

"What did you say?" Billy Dumphy demanded, coming right up to Tad's face, daring him to repeat it. The words stuck in his throat for an instant. Somehow they seemed different now, as if, by saying them again, he'd be challenging the shadow house on the hill and everything in the night around it.

"I—could," Tad managed again.

"Oh, yeah, Gorman." Billy's grin twisted into a sneer. "Right. Sure." He leaned closer still, his nose almost touching Tad's. "Then I dare you. I double-dare you. I goddamn triple dare you, you faggot. You don't even have the guts to walk up on the porch."

Tad looked around at the others, his friends, the guys he played stickball with. The guys who played kick the can. All the kids with their caps pulled down over their foreheads, half of them wearing shirts a size too large, handed down from fathers or older brothers; some of them with arms or legs a little too long, waiting for the rest of their bodies to hurry up and grow; all the kids that looked just like him.

They all stared back at him. None of them said a single word. It was up to Tad now.

It was like he was in a tunnel with only two ways out. He could take what he said back, and the others would probably never talk to him again. Or he could do it. He could go inside that stupid house.

Billy wouldn't let it go. "So what are you going to do, faggot?"

One of the other guys snickered. It was getting darker. A cold breeze had sprung up off the lake.

He heard other voices, just up the street. Billy waved for all the others to duck down behind the bushes.

Six people walked though the gate of the Stauf place. They climbed the path toward the front door.

Tad felt a sharp jab in his ribs.

"There!" Billy called in a hoarse voice just above a whisper. "You won't be alone, Gorman. There's a whole bunch of people going in the house."

Old Henry Stauf's house. The toymaker. Everyone Tad knew had a Henry Stauf toy at home. So what if you never saw anybody going in or out of Old Man Stauf's place? What could be so bad about a house built by a toymaker?

"So what the hell's it going to be, Gorman?" Billy insisted.

"I'll do it," Tad heard himself say. The other kids sucked in their breath. "I said I could—and I will."

Billy still wouldn't let it rest. "Yeah. But the dare means that you'll go through the whole house. All the rooms. Not just a quick in and out, like a rabbit."

Tad nodded. He watched the other people walk into the house.

I won't be alone, he thought. There will be other people there. I won't be alone.

"Go on." One of the kids giggled. Somebody gave Tad a push. "Go on."

Tad stood. The evening breeze pushed against him, making his sweat-stained shirt stick to his back. The kids had been hanging around out here since dinner. It was getting dark. His father would be calling him to come in soon.

How long would it take to look at a crummy old house? He'd get Billy Dumphy to eat his words.

He started towards the house. The other kids' voices faded behind him as he climbed up the path. He thought he saw more than one pair of glowing eyes, watching him from the bushes as he passed.

There are other people inside already, he thought. How bad can it be?

His footsteps sounded hollow as he climbed the worn front steps. He couldn't just go in the front door. That's where those six adults had gone. He might be happy they were in there, but he would just as soon get in and out of the place before they knew he was around.

He turned left, walking across the porch that ran the entire length of the house. Maybe he could find an open window.

The first room he peered into was a dining room, with places set for seven people.

The next window looked into the kitchen. A giant metal pot sat on the stove. He smelled something, even through the window. It made his nostrils twitch. The kitchen was small, with a door leading over to a cupboard off to one side.

The window was closed tight, but there was a place at the window's bottom where a bit of the frame had rotted away. If he could just get his fingers in there, he might be able to open the window from the outside.

He managed to cram the tips of both hands into the narrow space, so that his fingers were touching the window's lower edge. He pulled upwards, but the window wouldn't budge.

He took a deep breath and tried again. The window gave half an inch.

He heard voices from somewhere inside. He froze, his hands still on the window.

The voices drifted away.

He pushed again, and the window gave a couple more inches. Another tug, and the opening looked big enough for him to stick his head through.

He pushed his head and shoulders through the opening, then kicked off with his feet, arms cushioning his fall, sliding into the kitchen like a snake.

The smell from the pot was far stronger in here. It made Tad want to gag. It didn't smell like anything he had ever eaten—or would ever want to eat.

He turned back to the window. Best to close it, to remove any evidence that he had passed this way.

The window slammed shut with barely a touch. Why did he have the feeling it wouldn't open again?

Somewhere behind him, deeper in the house, he heard a woman scream.

Dutton heard the screams, and the answering shouts as someone rushed to the woman's rescue. Dutton was alone. Somehow, they had all split up. He wondered if Stauf had something to do with that, too.

He was beginning to think that nothing here happened by chance. Stauf was somewhere nearby, watching everything.

Stauf would expect everybody to run towards the screams. Or maybe that was the point—maybe Stauf was looking for someone who wouldn't follow the crowd, who would go off on his own no matter what was going on with the others. It was certainly worth a try. So Dutton kept on walking in the opposite direction, down the hall and up the stairs to the second floor.

Five of the rooms up here sported name plates, one for the two Knoxes and one each for the remaining guests. He quickly walked down the hall to the room with his name on it and turned the knob. At least this door opened with ease.

The room was totally dark, and the dim light from the hallway did little to penetrate the gloom. Dutton felt along the wall for a light switch, but there was none on the right hand side of the door. He moved his hand toward the left.

And he heard music.

It was distant at first. A choir singing. But it seemed to become louder with every passing note, as if the choir were somewhere in the house and moving closer to the spot where Dutton stood.

Could the noise be coming from the hall? Somehow, the door had closed behind him. He felt for the knob, but couldn't find the door, the wall, anything. He now felt as if he stood in the middle of a great, cavernous space. And it sounded as if the choir were in this place with him.

The choir half-chanted, half sang in some language Dutton had never heard before. But, if they were walking through this room around him, why weren't there any lights to guide them?

The singing became louder still. Dutton thought about calling out, to try and tell them someone else was here.

Frankly, the singing was now so loud he doubted he would be heard.

And it grew louder still, impossibly loud, as if the choir had invaded his skull. His head throbbed with the music; the chords reverberated in his bones; his eardrums would burst with the volume.

Why is this happening? Dutton thought. This did not sound anything like the secrets Stauf talked about in the letter. He covered his ears in a vain attempt to ease the pain. Had the mad toymaker simply lured his guests here to kill them, one by one?

Dutton screamed, the song so loud now it would surely tear his head apart.

And then there was light, and the sound was gone.

Julia Heine had gone upstairs to get some rest. The wine, while bitter, had been very potent. It seemed a good time to find her room and have a few minutes of peace and quiet.

But she hadn't been in there for five minutes when she heard the screams.

She sat on the bed for a long moment, until she was quite sure the screams were real. Sometimes, with alcohol, she'd been know to see and hear things that weren't really there. But the cries had kept on, and she had gone to investigate.

She didn't have to go far. The screams were coming from the very next room. She pounded on the door, but got no response.

She pushed the door open, taking a step away in case there was something dangerous on the other side.

But there was nothing, nothing but Brian Dutton, holding tight to his head as if it might burst.

Brian stopped mid-scream to stare at Julia.

There was no other sound.

Elinor had no voice left to scream.

But the blood wouldn't stop. It dripped down on her, drop after drop. Her head, her dress, her whole body would be covered in blood.

"No—" was all she could say. "No."

The thing had her ankle.

"No!" she moaned.

"Elinor, stop! What are you crying about?"

She blinked, then looked up. It was her husband. Edward had come to save her! She lifted her hands to show him the blood. But there was no blood there. Her hands and clothes were damp, nothing more.

Edward gave her his hand, and pulled her up from the basement floor. Another drop—of water—splattered on Elinor's forehead.

"Mr. Temple?"

He didn't want to look away.

The moment he took his eyes from that thing it would crash through the glass doors and devour them all. Or perhaps it didn't need to break down the doors at all. Perhaps it was only waiting to ooze through the smallest little crack, flowing through the spaces around the door frame so that it could devour everything in the room beyond.

"Mr. Temple!" the voice said again.

He turned away at last and saw the young woman, Martine, standing, looking at him. But she didn't look frightened in the least. If anything, she appeared amused.

Couldn't she see?

"Eh—Mr. Temple? Is there anything wrong?"

He pointed to the doors, unable to find the words.

He pointed and looked back to the thing that was coming for them. But nothing leaned against the doors.

There was only a light fog out there in the garden. The doors were covered with tiny, jewel-like drops of rain.

There was no shape pressing against the glass. Nothing else.

Stauf, Temple thought. This was the first of his tricks.

But it had been so real. So terrifying.

Magic, Temple realized. And he suspected this was only the first trick of many.

The words "opening moves" came to mind.

He turned back to Martine Burden, who shook her head, smiling, as if she was still waiting for him to share a joke.

When he managed to speak to her, his voice was a parched whisper.

"Get the others. We must talk."

Stauf was extremely proud of his house. In addition to the lavish rooms, there were secret entryways, hidden corridors, and many very special devices, all in preparation for this night. This *party*, he corrected himself, for that was what it had said on the invitation to his guests. He hadn't told them how different a party it would be, or how it would only be fun for one.

He wondered how many would guess his true purpose before they died?

He watched them now, and heard them, too, eavesdropping with the help of his special toys. The guests danced so readily to his tunes. He could not be more happy if they were puppets and he was pulling their strings. Even though they had stepped into the house only moments before, Stauf felt sure his new guests wouldn't disappoint him. After all, he'd chosen each and every one of them very specifically.

He was careful, first and foremost, to choose people in difficult situations. That sort of information came easily to a man with Stauf's resources. He had known—before any of the invitations had even been sent—that all of his guests were desperate, each in his or her own way; so desperate that they would see Stauf's invitation as a godsend, their last hope perhaps, and rush to attend.

And how were his six guests faring? He glanced from room to room, almost as if perusing a menu. Ah, there were

Edward and Elinor Knox—the loving couple. Except that Edward was so full of himself he couldn't see anybody else, while Elinor was totally dependent upon him, expecting Edward to do everything for her but breathe. Together, they were the perfect victims, ready for sacrifice. After all, someone had to show the others the way.

And who was this sashaying down the hall but the lovely Martine Burden? Before Stauf became wealthy, so many women had turned him away, scorned him, laughed in his face. Women just like the lovely Martine, covered with the trappings of society. Why should they even glance at a pitiful specimen like Stauf in their quest for wealth and power?

Stauf chuckled. He would show Martine what true power was.

And who follows Martine into the room but Brian Dutton—the ultimate businessman. Brian probably didn't even remember how, when Stauf had first opened his toy store, he promised then failed to deliver most of the store's shelves and fixtures. This time, Stauf would make sure the deal got done. Stauf always delivered. Before their little party was over, he'd get Brian to sell everything, even his soul.

Julia Heine lurched through the doorway. He had a special affection for Julia. He saw her as something of a female counterpart to the Stauf that once had been, before the voices had come and changed his life forever. He'd have to do something special for Julia before the party was over.

And, perhaps most of all, Hamilton Temple, who had made success out of illusion. How Stauf had envied the easy grace Temple had once used to make things appear and disappear at will. Stauf would throw magic back in Temple's face. In this place, Stauf decided what was real.

The final game had begun. And, assessing the competition, Stauf was supremely confident of victory.

Sixteen

Hamilton Temple stood with his back to the glass doors that had seemed—only minutes ago—to be a portal for some creature from a nightmare world.

From the looks on some of the others' faces, he was not the only one to have such an unsettling experience. Elinor Knox sat close by her husband. Her face pale, she couldn't keep her eyes off her Edward. Julia Heine sat in a wing chair sipping wine and smoking cigarettes, as if these two things could fill her entire world. Martine Burden paced about the room, studying the trick bookshelves. Occasionally, she would actually find a real book, which she removed and tossed to the ground. The faces she made as the others talked indicated that she considered all of this a waste of time.

Brian Dutton stood by the fireplace, quietly telling his story: "—on and on and on, filling my head. I heard singing upstairs—like a mad choir!"

Julia Heine made a barking noise, half cough, half laugh. "I heard nothing. Just you—in your room. Yelling like a crazy man."

Dutton stared back at Julia, half angry, half confused, as though he didn't know what to believe.

"And I saw blood," Elinor whispered, gripping hard at her husband's hand.

Her husband pulled away at that. Edward was the one who had found his wife. From his disdainful expression, Knox apparently hadn't seen any blood at all.

Martine paused in her pacing to smile at Knox. "How ghastly," she intoned.

Knox shook his head and smiled back, like they were just a couple of regular folks humoring their high-strung fellow guests.

Temple cleared his throat to get the other's attention.

"And I—" he began. "Well, I don't know how to describe what I saw." He waved towards the glass doors, as though they might help him explain. "Let me just suggest that none of you want to see it. It was too—"

Julia Heine stood up, rolling her eyes towards the ceiling. "And the rest of us saw absolutely nothing. How boring." She brushed at her skirt. "I suggest we all have some dinner."

Knox stepped closer to Martine.

"I think we're meant to eat the soup." He might have been speaking to everyone, but his gaze rested firmly on the woman in red.

The two of them seemed to take every opportunity they could get to talk or exchange glances. At the moment, Elinor appeared too upset to notice. Perhaps her husband did this sort of thing all the time. Right now, Temple thought they had more serious things to worry about.

There had to be some sort of pattern in all of this. Why were some of them exposed to the tricks of the house, some of Stauf's special surprises, while the others saw— and felt—nothing? For a moment there, he and Dutton and Elinor had all felt like they were in Hell. And he was afraid that this was only the beginning of Stauf's real plan, that something worse was waiting for all of them.

A couple of the other guests seemed to be drifting back towards the hallway. How could he get them to take their situation seriously?

"Wait!" Temple called after them. "We should have some rules. We should team up, stay together."

Martine spared him a withering glance. "Don't be a bore, darling."

Edward Knox laughed at that, the life of the party. "It's a *game*. That's why we were invited. A game! Every one for himself—" he smiled over at Martine "—or herself. Crazy old Stauf is watching us, scaring us. Watching us play at his puzzles. Only he knows the rules."

Temple could do nothing but stare back at the chubby, self-satisfied Knox. The man had no imagination—a failing that might be the death of someone in a place like this. But Knox and Martine couldn't take their eyes off each other. They had other things on their mind than Mr. Stauf.

Temple had to explain the danger here, had to make them see. But no one had the time, all of them had turned away. No one seemed to take him seriously; proceeding with dinner was so much more important than planning to save their lives.

Temple supposed this was the way it had to be. They all had their reasons for staying. That no doubt was why Stauf picked them in the first place. For many of them this place promised them money, or power, or maybe even a little sex. They would not give up their dreams easily, even if a nightmare or two stood in their way.

But none of the others wanted to work together. And certainly none of them wanted to leave. Temple had to admit that he didn't want to leave either. Part of him actually wanted to stay even more than before. These "unexplained occurrences" so many of them had experienced might be real magic after all.

But he was even more convinced that, simply because they had been invited into Stauf's house, they needn't play along with the toymaker. Perhaps he could speak to some of the others individually, somehow get them to see reason, explain to them how much better their chances would be if they worked together.

No doubt Stauf had many secrets. The more of them Temple and the others knew, the better their chances for survival.

None of them could fathom the true depth of their troubles; Stauf could have brought them here for anything, even murder. When Temple thought of it that way, Knox's last remark was even more chilling.

Only Stauf knows the rules.

Julia Heine went to the kitchen and sniffed at the big metal pot. She had turned the heat off beneath the soup just before she'd joined the others in the library. It was now no longer simmering, but the soup still smelled very warm and very appetizing. She took a deep breath, her mouth watering. Either Stauf was quite a cook himself, or he hired the very best. Not that their host or any of his servants had bothered to show themselves. Julia wondered what the guests might have to do to gain that sort of honor.

She looked around the kitchen. It was outfitted with a good collection of pots and pans, but seemed a bit small and crowded for a house of this size, the large ovens and counterspace so overwhelming that there was hardly room to walk. And then — she turned around.

She saw an open pantry behind her, filled with shelves and shelves of cans and boxed goods.

Julia frowned. There was something odd about the way all these multicolored packages were bunched together on the shelves, lit by a single light overhead that made them stand out against the dark wood of the surrounding walls. They seemed to form a sort of pattern. Another one of Stauf's puzzles, she thought? Especially with all those cans on the upper shelves, each marked with a single letter. There was a message here somewhere; all those letters could form words. Perhaps they needed to be arranged in a special pattern.

She wished she had brought her glass of wine with her. Alcohol always helped her wipe away her troubles and focus her thoughts. Still, perhaps she could solve a bit of this puzzle first and fetch her wine later.

She pulled one can free and replaced it with another, then a second and a third, always careful to keep the spacing of the cans the same. The pattern had to be part of the puzzle.

Yes, the cans could form words, the words a sentence. She frowned, concentrating on rearranging the letters. It all made sense after a fashion.

"Yes," she murmured to herself, "this is it. This—no, not quite—" She almost giggled. She was going to solve one of Henry Stauf's puzzles.

But what happened if she solved it? Stauf's note hadn't been very clear on that. Now that she thought about it, the note hadn't actually been very clear on anything. At the very least, she should get a prize.

The words fell into place as she moved the final can.

"There!" she announced to the world. "I've solved the puzzle!"

The pot bubbled behind her.

But the heat had been turned off, hadn't it?

Julia turned back to the stove.

That was closer than Tad wanted.

He had explored most of the first floor by now, looking for some way—any way—to get out of this place; every room but the one where all the other people were having that meeting. But there were a couple of doors on this floor that wouldn't open, and the front door was securely locked. None of the other windows would budge, either. So he had come back here, to the kitchen, hoping to use the same window he'd come in through.

But the lady walked in almost right behind him, so close she had practically stumbled over him.

Not that she noticed. She looked like she had been drinking. All she seemed to want to do was stand in the cupboard and keep moving those stupid cans, talking to herself all the time.

She was completely occupied by those cans. At least it gave Tad a chance to get out of there. His shoes barely hit the linoleum as he snuck past her.

The more he explored this place, the more he thought you had to be crazy to set foot in a house like this. So the way the lady acted shouldn't surprise him at all. Just another creepy part of this crazy house.

Of course, what did that make *him*?

Trapped here, if he didn't find a way out. But he had tried most everything on this floor. He could hear some of the others moving around. That meeting must be over. They would be all over the place now. Every time he saw one of these crazy people, he wanted to meet them even less.

Where would he go?

He stepped from the kitchen into the hallway that connected all the rooms, looking across the entryway to the grand, curving staircase. It would only take an unlocked window, and a short drop to the porch below, to get out through the second floor. Maybe the way out waited for him upstairs.

Temple paced down the upstairs hall.

Each bedroom had a name on it. Six rooms lined the upstairs hallway, six doors with six name cards. And there were the usual locked doors. Stauf did like to keep his secrets.

But there was a seventh room, too, a room without a name. Temple had opened that door first to see the room was filled, floor to ceiling, with games. It would be a very special room for the likes of Henry Stauf; it deserved further exploration. First, though, he'd return to the hallway and find the door with his name on it.

The nameplates seemed surprisingly considerate, especially seeing how little other hospitality they had received from their absent host. At least Stauf doesn't want us to guess about everything, Temple thought. Of course, placing specific people in specific bedrooms might be a part of Stauf's master plan. If Stauf had a master plan. Temple sighed. There were too many questions.

And only Stauf had the answers.

He looked down the hall and saw Elinor Knox standing alone. Her husband had disappeared. It came as no surprise to the magician that he hadn't seen Martine Burden for the last few minutes, either.

He walked up behind Mrs. Knox. She just stared at the closed door before her, lost in her thoughts. He felt he should say something to announce his presence.

"This must be your room," he said, pointing to the small card affixed to the door.

Elinor Knox looked up dully, as if all the emotion had been drained from her by her recent experience. "I—I don't want to go in," she admitted after a moment's hesitation. "I'm still—shaky."

Temple smiled. No more than I am, he thought but didn't say. That was the kind of agreement Elinor Knox didn't need just now.

"There's nothing to be scared of," he replied. "Just Stauf's tricks." The words sounded reassuring. He just didn't know if they were true. Maybe he was saying them to calm himself as much as Mrs. Knox.

She placed her hand on the doorknob and pushed the door open a crack. She looked back to Temple. "Will you be in your room?"

"Yes. Or the game room." Temple pointed down the hall to the open door.

He turned to go, but Elinor called after him, as if she were desperate not to be left alone.

"We all want something," she said quickly. "That's why we're here, isn't it?"

"I suppose so." Temple smiled.

"What do you want?" Elinor persisted.

Temple glanced away for an instant. What was his real reason for being here? What was his innermost desire? He hadn't known that he would ever choose to admit this. He laughed. "Not much. Just—I've been a stage magician all my life. And I'd like to know—is there any real magic? Does Stauf know that? Can he give that to me. . . ."

It all sounded a little silly to him now, as he said it aloud. But Elinor Knox didn't seem to notice. Instead, she turned away and spoke in turn.

"I—we—need some way out, some way to start our life again. Edward has gotten us in such debt. There's no money and . . ." Her voice drifted off as she shook her head.

Interesting, Temple thought, that she spoke about her husband's problems, as if his needs took precedence over any of her own. He wondered what Elinor Knox really wanted for herself—if she could admit to wanting anything.

"And what about the others?" she asked.

Temple frowned. What did the others really want?

"I don't know." Temple suspected what their motivations might be, but he would like to let them speak for themselves—if they ever got the chance.

And who knew what their chances were? They were all waiting for Stauf to make the next move.

SEVENTEEN

Deciding to examine his own bedroom, Temple strode down the hall to the room with his nameplate, wondering what other surprises their absent host might have in store.

When he opened the door and stepped inside, his first reaction was to laugh.

He had stepped into the room looking for some new puzzle or game, some clue to Stauf's master plan. He had even readied himself for another of Stauf's nightmare images, although, for the moment at least, those seemed to be distributed one to a customer.

He had never expected this. The place looked like a magic museum, with display cases filled with the paraphernalia of the trade, from cards to capes to chains. Ah, but the *piece de resistance*, the crowning achievement of the whole room, was the decoration on the bedroom walls. Here, framed and lovingly preserved behind glass, were posters of Hamilton Temple's greatest triumphs.

"FOR FOUR WEEKS ONLY AT THE ODEAN!"

"SEE A WOMAN SAWED IN HALF!"

"REVEALED AT LAST—THE MYSTERY OF THE ANCIENT SPHINX!"

"HELD OVER!"

"SEE THE AMAZING INDIAN ROPE TRICK!"

"RECENTLY RETURNED FROM A TOUR BEFORE THE CROWNED HEADS OF EUROPE!"

"SEE HAMILTON TEMPLE CHEAT DEATH!"

Temple was surprised at how pleased he was to see these pieces of his personal history. He hadn't seen a number of these posters in years. He was amazed that some of them still existed. The hoopla on some of these things did stretch the truth a bit, like that one about the "Crowned Heads of Europe." He had performed a couple of weeks in London's East End, and one night someone said a baron or some such was in the audience. That was as close as Temple had ever gotten to a crown.

But why were all these posters and other paraphernalia here?

This incredibly decorated room could almost be a shrine to Temple's career. Temple knew Stauf had almost unlimited amounts of money, and with those funds he seemed to have scoured the country, maybe even the world, looking for souvenirs from the life of Hamilton Temple.

He guessed everybody needed a hobby, and it looked like Stauf's hobby was Hamilton Temple.

But why? Why go to such lengths for a man Stauf had never met? Was all this a measure of respect, or of jealousy? Did he consider Temple a fellow practitioner of an exotic craft, or a competitor, someone to be challenged and bested in a tour of magical might?

Temple wondered if anything in this room might give him some answers.

He lifted a set of chains. When Temple was younger, he used to perform elaborate escapes as the finale to his show. Perhaps, long ago, Stauf had been a member of Temple's audience.

"Sturdy work," Hamilton murmured as he rattled the chains. "Even Houdini didn't use such a heavy weight—" These chains, in fact, might be too sturdy to use in an escape act; Temple wondered how many classic magic tricks Stauf actually knew.

He placed the chains back on the table and walked over to the display case on the far side of the bed. There, on the top of the case, was a magician's top hat, the sort Temple had used early in his career, before he had decided that a turban looked much more mysterious.

Ah, the magic hat. For many stage magicians, this, along with perhaps a magic wand, was the most important tool. On a whim, Temple removed his turban and tried the hat on for size. It was, of course, a perfect fit.

Temple touched the hat on his head. "Perhaps," he said with a laugh, "this is the secret to Stauf's power."

Temple hesitated. He had felt something when he touched the hat, a spark, like static electricity at first, until it flowed through his hand and arm to his torso.

Temple felt different, energized.

Perhaps this old top hat held some strange power after all.

He whirled about, looking around him. The room looked different now. Motes of light sparkled in the air, like waves of energy. Temple felt as if he might reach out and grab that energy and make it do whatever he wanted.

Hell, he was a magician, wasn't he? Maybe it was time to do a little magic.

But first he needed a beautiful assistant!

Brian Dutton had gone looking for voices. He had heard that choir once. He knew he would hear it again.

He walked slowly down the second floor corridor, looking and listening for anything out of the ordinary. But, instead of hearing a choir, he heard wild laughter.

It came from the bedroom across the hall from his own. The door was slightly ajar. He opened the door and stepped inside.

There, in the middle of the room, was Hamilton Temple, twirling about and laughing like an idiot.

"Temple?" Dutton called to the older man. "What's all the noise?"

But Hamilton Temple didn't answer. Instead, he reached both hands towards his bed. Dutton looked where Temple pointed. There, where there had been nothing a moment before, was a beautiful woman.

"Yes!" Temple shouted.

"Temple!" Dutton called again. "What the hell are you doing?"

But the old magician either couldn't hear Dutton, or didn't want to. He gestured toward the bed again, toward the alluring young woman who held her arms out to both the men. And she changed. She seemed to be growing older, ten years in ten seconds. Her face and hands wrinkled, her hair went from chestnut brown to silver.

But the change didn't stop there. The woman's body shriveled, her skin turning an unhealthy grey. She struggled for an instant, then fell back upon the bed as if dead. Holes appeared in her flesh as maggots crawled in and out.

Dutton wanted to run from the room. Why was Temple doing this? What did he hope to prove?

"Stop it!" Dutton called. "Stop what you're—"

But Temple seemed beyond hearing, as if whatever spell he had conjured had captured the magician as well.

The body of the woman on the bed began to split in two. A tremendous wind filled the room, coming not from the windows or the hall, but from inside the body. Pictures banged against the walls. From somewhere, Dutton heard the rattle of chains. Part of Dutton still wanted to leave, to get as far away from here as possible, but he found it impossible to move, as if his shoes were nailed to the floor.

And still the woman continued to split. Dutton thought he saw something, deep within the corpse, a moving shadow waiting for the body to be split in two, waiting to be free.

"No!" Dutton screamed, but his voice was lost to the wind.

But the thing, the moving shadow, was coming out.

Temple stood as rigid as a soldier, no longer slightly bent by age. He made a fist.

"Stop!" he called.

The wind died, and the woman was gone.

Dutton stared at Temple. Somehow, he felt as if they had barely survived something that in a few seconds would have become a catastrophe. What was happening here?

Hamilton Temple looked at the hat in his hands. It had fallen from his head the moment the woman—and whatever was inside her, trying to get out—had disappeared.

He blinked and shook his head, half in disbelief, half to clear his head. When had Dutton come into the room?

He had thought, at first, that he had been in control of the magic. He had been filled with a manic energy and was sure he could direct that energy wherever he wanted. But, as the scene unfolded, it began to seem more as if the magic, if that was what it was, had control of him.

It had begun well enough. He thought about a beautiful assistant, and there she was. But she began to age at a fantastic rate, only to have the flesh rot from her bones. For an instant, Temple thought he had done this as well—an errant thought perhaps, about the power of life and death, that instantly changed this creation of Stauf's magic hat.

But then the woman had begun to split in two, like some wild parody of sawing your assistant in half. Temple realized then that this apparition was beyond his control. And he saw, at the same time, lurking deep inside the woman, another of the nightmares that Stauf liked to spring upon his guests. Temple's emotions had rushed in all at once then. He had become terribly afraid, and just as determined that Stauf's nightmare would not come to pass.

Only when Temple had put a stop to the magic drama did he realize this was all Stauf's show, a little performance specifically for Temple's benefit. And, looking back at it now, he had to admit he found that show both wonderful and terrible.

He glanced over at Dutton, who was still staring at him open-mouthed, as if he had no idea what to believe. What exactly should the magician tell Mr. Dutton about all this? Exactly how far did Temple trust Dutton, after all?

Not very far, Temple decided.

"Mr. Stauf," Temple said with the lightest of smiles, "was just showing me a few new tricks."

"Those were tricks?" Dutton laughed, a nervous sound, totally without humor. "You've spoken with Mr. Stauf?"

Temple shook his head. "Only after a fashion. I've seen no more of Henry Stauf than anyone else. These tricks were left for me."

Dutton shook his own head in reply. "If these are only tricks, I don't think I want to get on the wrong side of our host."

Get on the wrong side of Henry Stauf? Temple looked at the hat now in his hand.

Something like that might not be helped. There was something in this magic, and in the visions he had seen in the library downstairs, that struck Temple as profoundly evil. He expected that Stauf would try to lure his guests into joining in that evil; evil, and maybe death. It was, Temple reflected, only by being on the wrong side of Stauf that some of them might survive.

Perhaps, Temple thought, he should share some of his concerns with Dutton after all. But, when he looked back toward the door where Dutton had stood, the other guest had already gone, intent on whatever errand he had been on before Temple's demonstration had interrupted him. An errand, no doubt, designed by Henry Stauf.

Temple looked back to the hat. Whatever power had been in this thing was gone now. It was, as he said, another of Stauf's tricks.

Henry Stauf obviously wanted to give Temple a taste of his power.

A taste, and a challenge. After all, Temple had controlled Stauf's spell at the end.

Temple would rise to Stauf's challenge. If there were truly magic here, Hamilton Temple would claim it for his own.

EIGHTEEN

nce she had actually opened the door and stepped inside, Elinor Knox had to admit that the bedroom was very nice. The place reserved for her and her husband was quite well appointed, even reassuring, filled with solid, dark furniture of very tasteful design. Some of the pieces in here—the delicate vases, the chest of drawers with a carved headboard and ornate brass knobs—were certainly antiques. She wished she and Edward could afford such fine things. She sighed. Perhaps, if they were able to resolve their debt with Stauf's help, they might even be able to buy such things—someday.

She looked down at the intricate, deep red carpet by the four-poster bed. It was a most unusual rug, with an elaborate pattern covering all but the outer fringes.

"This is so beautiful," she whispered, "and—" She frowned as she studied the intricate weave; the pattern—the grey, white, and black threads intermixed with the red—suddenly made a crazy sense. "It's a maze. I did something like this when I was a girl. You have to go . . ."

She knelt down by the carpet's edge and began to trace the way through the maze with her fingers, following one passageway after another. All her attention was on those fingers as they reached the heart of the maze, as if the maze might draw her inside, and she would be walking down narrow corridors with high, featureless walls.

"... all the way to the center."

She blinked. The walls were gone. She had solved the maze, and somehow the spell was broken. She pulled her gaze away from the carpet and sat back on the bed. This entire evening had been so exhausting, and it had barely begun.

Something brushed her cheek, so gently that it might have been a breeze.

She looked up. A young man was standing by the bedside—a quite handsome young man in his early twenties, dressed as if he might have stepped out of a picture book published a hundred years ago.

Elinor shrank back on the bed. "Who the devil are you?"

The handsome young man smiled down at her.

"A friend—your friend. You are looking for a friend, aren't you?"

She stared up at this strange young man. His smile was so warm. This whole evening had been so tiring, and so confusing. Could this be the other guest Stauf was waiting for?

And what about his question?

Was she looking for a friend? Well, she had certainly confided in Hamilton Temple, who seemed a kind and caring fellow, despite that silly costume he wore. She had found Mr. Temple very reassuring, especially after that upsetting event in the basement.

But was she looking for more than reassurance?

She had always found her reassurance in Edward, for all these many long years of their marriage. Oh, he could be short with her sometimes, and their marriage was not always all that it could be. But she had learned to depend on Edward and their marriage—until tonight.

Edward and Elinor, Elinor and Edward, and now Edward was gone, heaven knew where. It was like, after they had stepped into this house, her husband had become a stranger. It had been so long since she had really thought about what she herself wanted. She certainly didn't want to be alone.

The handsome stranger sat down beside her. She was surprised that she didn't back away.

"You feel alone here, don't you?" the stranger asked.

Yes, she thought, more than anything else. It was like this strange young man could read her thoughts. And what did she feel about him?

She had always had feelings about people that had helped to direct her life—what Edward called her "spells." She had had a very bad feeling about Stauf's invitation and had come only because her husband insisted. But since she had gotten here, she had felt nothing, as if all those good and bad sensations were somehow hidden from her.

It was the same with this stranger. She looked at him, and at first felt nothing at all.

And how did she really feel? About herself?

She felt more alone than she had in her entire life.

"Yes," she admitted.

The man smiled back at her, a warm and innocent smile. "We can be together."

Was this what she was really looking for? Someone who really cared for her, someone who would devote his entire life, his entire being, to what she wanted; all her needs, spiritual, financial, physical—

No! What was she thinking about? What about Edward? She was a married woman. This was all wrong. She couldn't forget all those years together.

"Forever," the handsome stranger whispered.

Suddenly, he kissed her. She closed her eyes, but she didn't pull away. How long had it been since she had felt such a kiss?

How long had it been since Edward had kissed her?

She opened her eyes and saw the handsome stranger staring intently back at her.

"You must do something for me."

Before she knew it, he leaned over and whispered in her ear.

She was so confused. He was so close. What had that kiss meant?

What had he said? She was so overwhelmed by this stranger's presence, by this stranger's kiss, she had barely heard the words.

He had spoken of death.

And whom she had to kill.

His touch was no longer gentle. The stranger gripped her shoulder hard, as if he might force her to do the things he wanted. He grinned at her reaction, happy at her revulsion. She pulled back, but his hand merely moved down to her upper arm. The fingers dug painfully into her flesh. He chuckled at her pain.

"Let me go!" she screamed. "God, no! Let me go!"

She tried to twist away from the hand that held her. But it was no longer a hand. It had somehow turned into a vine: a long tendril, grey-green and ragged, curling around her arm. The thorns tore at her skin like fingers, hundreds of tiny claws ready to draw blood, as the vine reached to encircle her neck.

She screamed and tried to pull herself from the bed. But another vine gripped one of her legs and was rising up to wrap her torso. The vines would strangle her where she lay.

This was so crazy, so unreal, she realized, just like other things that had happened in this house.

"No!" she screamed again. "This isn't happening!" It had to be a fake, just like that blood in the basement, some sort of trick to frighten her.

She couldn't fight what wasn't real.

And then the vine changed again, transforming itself into something that at least looked human.

But the stranger was no longer young. Old and bald, he leered at her, liquor heavy on his breath, as he pulled her towards a closer embrace.

She had seen this man before, in that toy shop in the middle of town.

It was Henry Stauf.

Elinor found herself almost overwhelmed by emotion as all the very worst of her "feelings" came flooding back. This was the true nature of Stauf, the true secret of this place, an evil staggering in its strength. She had never felt such a loathsome vileness before. Somehow, Stauf had hidden the evil from her until he was so close there could be no more secrets. No more secrets and maybe no more life. What did he plan to do to her, to Edward, to all the others?

And then Stauf disappeared.

Elinor Knox was all alone.

Martine Burden's bedroom was pink and red. Female sort of colors, Edward Knox thought, colors especially suited to a woman like Martine.

Wonderful colors, perhaps. But what was he doing here? He felt immensely uncomfortable as she pulled him into the room and shut the door. He had other things to do and places to be. He had come to this place for a reason. What would his wife do without him?

Martine looked into Edward's eyes. She had such an intensity about her; it was almost enough to make him forget his discomfort and all his responsibilities.

"You know the others will try to beat us." Her voice was low and husky, barely more than a whisper.

He nodded. Others? Was she saying that she wanted them— Martine and Edward—to work together? But he barely heard her words. He was watching the way her eyes flashed in the light, how her full lips shaped the syllables, the way her body moved as she pulled him towards the bed.

"But that doesn't have to happen," Martine continued. "Not if you and I work together." Her hands stroked his arms, promising an even deeper partnership than her words.

"We can solve Stauf's puzzles. We can win." She stepped close, looking straight into his eyes. "You can get what you want, Edward."

Another step. She brought her hands up to his shoulders. She touched his neck. They were beautiful hands, the fingers so slender and cool. "And what is it you want, Edward?"

He looked deep into Martine's eyes. She could make a man want her, Edward knew. He felt everything slip away, everything but those eyes, that face, that beautiful female form.

The slightest of smiles graced her lips. "Should I try to guess?"

Edward knew she could see right through him, see the sweat on his brow, see the desire in his eyes.

She pulled him close to kiss him. And he kissed her back. In that instant, he didn't care about anything except the woman before him.

She pulled away from him, then. "I know where the puzzle is that we must solve."

What was she saying? What did it matter? She had her hands on his lapels. And she was pulling him toward the bed.

"I know where it is," she murmured.

A puzzle, she said.

"I'll take you there," she added.

Edward Knox wanted to solve only one puzzle, the one that involved a man and a woman.

"But first—" She pulled him down next to her on the bed.

His head was filled with her perfume, her perfume and the odd musk that filled the room. He had not felt this sort of desire in years.

He would do anything for a woman like Martine.

She kissed him again and stripped off his clothes.

"I can give you what you want," she whispered. "I can give you—what you want—"

Edward Knox could do nothing but agree.

NINETEEN

Tad saw the lady through the open door.

She was tracing a pattern on the carpet by the bed. She stopped suddenly and looked up as if someone had spoken to her. For an instant, Tad thought she'd seen him, but she was looking and talking to someone in the room. Except Tad could see the rest of the room, and there was nobody there.

It was like that woman down in the kitchen. Maybe everybody was going crazy.

Maybe, Tad thought, it was something about the house. Maybe it would try to make him crazy, too.

He had to be careful. Crazy people could do anything.

Tad crept away from the lady talking to no one. She didn't look his way once.

Before, when he first broke into the house, he had just been worried about somebody telling his dad and the walloping he'd get. He wasn't supposed to come anywhere near the old Stauf house.

Now Tad was starting to think he'd rather have the walloping than whatever was going to happen here.

Crazy people could do anything. Maybe he should get away from everyone and hide until morning.

At the end of the hall, a narrow staircase led up, to an attic, Tad guessed. Maybe that would be the best place to hide.

He walked quietly down the hall towards the stairs, until he came to another open door. But this wasn't a bedroom. This room was filled with games.

Something in Tad wanted to stop right here. He had to go and take a look.

Maybe, if he had to hide, he could take something interesting with him; something he could fool around with until morning.

He stepped inside.

Temple carefully surveyed the game room. You couldn't call it anything else, for games and puzzles occupied every available inch of space atop the furniture, and on great shelves that lined the walls. He saw the usual things, classic games from checkers and chess to the Indian game of *pachisi* and the Chinese game of *Go*. There were commercial games, too, bright boxes with titles like *Journey to the Arctic* and *Cop the Kaiser*. But there were far stranger things on some of the shelves, games and puzzles no doubt built by Stauf, fairly simple devices upon the lower levels, but increasingly more elaborate as the shelves rose toward the ceiling. Stauf's skill, and his games, had improved over time.

"The mad man's playroom," Temple said aloud, mostly to break the silence in this strange place. But this place would truly be worth exploring. This room would be closer to the toymaker's heart than any other. This room could easily hold the toymaker's secrets.

"Tell me, mad man," he addressed the room. "Can you give me real magic?"

He thought about what had happened in his bedroom only a few moments ago. Had that been magic? It had certainly been marvelous, especially for those few brief moments when Hamilton Temple believed he was in control.

But, upon reflection, he felt more like the audience than the magician, a mere observer of all the marvels Henry Stauf provided. Stauf had given him that alluring woman on the bed, who was there only to split in two, revealing some far darker power beneath.

Temple had just barely been able to stop that power—and not, he was sure, before Stauf gave him a glimpse of exactly what the toymaker wanted him to see.

Power. Almost limitless power, coming from someplace very dark, someplace very far away.

But was this power truly magic? Or was it something else masquerading as magic?

That was why Temple would stay. He needed to find the source of Stauf's power, and whether it was true magic or not.

It might be the last great gamble of his life. In fact, he was betting his life on it.

He walked across the room, looking from game to puzzle to game, searching for some insight into the toymaker's soul.

He spoke aloud again, as if the toymaker would answer. "Can you show me—"

His voice died as he stopped at the chessboard on the far side of the room. Seven pieces stood on the board, intricately carved;—so intricate that he could see details on the faces.

And the faces were theirs, the chess pieces carved to represent the six guests that had come to Stauf's mansion tonight. The bishop had Temple's head, turban and all. Dutton was a knight, Edward Knox a rook, Martine and Elinor were Queens, Julia a mere pawn.

And the king? Temple picked up the seventh piece and stared at it. The face carved here looked like that of a boy, a child.

Was this the seventh guest?

"No," Temple whispered. Stauf and his strange house had already captured the six of them. It was quite likely it would destroy them, too. But the six adults had come here by their own choice, led by their own foolish desires.

That wasn't enough for Stauf and the power behind him.

"Now they want the boy."

He stared at the chess piece. To trap a boy, a mere child, into whatever mad plan Stauf had concocted—it was horrible. Temple had visions of children crying, children sick, confused, clutching their toys as life slipped away from them. And Stauf had done all this. The toymaker didn't care what he did to children, so long as it gave him his magic.

Killing children. As a magician, Temple had spent most of his life performing for children, trying to show them that there might be magic in this world. But Henry Stauf had been a toymaker. He had made things to give children joy. How could he turn around then and destroy them? Temple felt tears streaming down his face at the very thought of it.

"No," Temple cried, his voice rising with emotion, "damn you, you can't—"

He stopped abruptly.

The boy—a real boy, his face identical to that on the chess piece—stared at Temple from the other side of the room.

TWENTY

He has many questions. The house is all too familiar. He walks the halls, and sees the ghosts of those who have gone before. A woman in white flees down the hallway before him. Hands press out from inside a picture, desperate to escape.

There are ghosts all around him. The boy and the other guests, so alive one minute, seem to fade the next, translucent spirits doomed to walk these halls by his side, over and over again. It is as if the house, and the guests, have been here forever, and will be here forever more.

Has he been here forever, too?

It seems to him now that all of it, all of the drama, all of the deaths, are playing themselves out over and over again, all under the watchful gaze of Henry Stauf.

As soon as the thought comes to him, he is certain it is true. The builder of this house, the mad toymaker, is behind it all. He realizes then that Stauf is the key to everything. In a house full of secrets, this is the most important of them all. When he finds Stauf, he will remember why he is here as well.

But why doesn't Stauf show himself? Why is he hiding?

As if in answer, he hears the song the children sing again and again, from where they always seem to stand, just beyond the iron gate.

Except, this time, the song is a bit different. He stops and listens to the words. Maybe they will reveal what he has been seeking for so long:

> "Old Man Stauf built a house,
> And filled it with his toys.
> Seven guests all came one night;
> Their screams the only noise.
>
> "Blood inside the library,
> Blood right down the hall,
> Blood going up the attic stairs
> Where the last guest did fall.
>
> "The last was just a little boy
> Dared to sneak at night
> But he was the key to the madman's door
> He released the evil's might.
>
> "Not one soul came out that night.
> No one was ever seen.
> But Old Mad Stauf is waiting there,
> Crazy, sick and mean . . ."

There is a new verse. The one about the boy. And releasing evil's might.

Somehow, he feels the children are singing it just for him.

He pauses in his search of the house to look in a mirror. No one looks back at him. Instead, he sees dim lights shining in darkness, lights that seem to be part of something much larger, like great shapes are crowding about the other side of the mirror. And all those shapes want to come through the mirror to join him.

No. They want to do things that are far worse than that. They are things that do not belong in this world. Stauf is bringing them.

It is all coming back to him; as if, again, it has happened many times before.

He remembers now.

He has the answer.

He knows what must be done.

TWENTY-ONE

artine Burden led the way. That was just the way she wanted it.

She pressed the panel by the side of the door and the once-locked door swung open, revealing a room full of paintings. The portrait gallery, she guessed one would call it. Not that you would want to meet many of the people shown in these portraits.

"I saw this room before," she said as she pulled Edward Knox into the room after her. She was barely able to contain her excitement. "And I know what this is."

But Edward pulled away from her hand to look at all the paintings around them.

"Strange paintings," he muttered, shaking his head in disapproval. "Sick."

Martine sighed, ever so softly. Poor Edward. He was so impressionable. He had almost been too easy to seduce.

Martine knew she would tire of him soon. But, once they had won Stauf's little game and were out of this madhouse, she could always turn the tables and leave him for someone else. After taking all the money, of course. It would be awfully easy to do. After all, Edward trusted her.

Still, she needed him now. He would protect her. And, if someone had to die, Edward Knox would be first in line as well. And Martine would tag along for the reward. She would reap all the benefits with none of the risk, the same way she planned to run the entire rest of her life.

She decided she should give Edward a moment to look around the room. As malleable as he was, Edward was a little slow and stodgy as well. He needed time to adjust. Every man came with his own disadvantages. Martine simply had to learn how to take advantage of them.

Even she admitted that the paintings were very bizarre, as if Stauf collected nothing but artwork that distorted life. They were surrounded by great tableaus filled with fantasy figures and portraits that turned their subjects into freaks. Unless, Martine considered, the subjects had been freaks in the first place.

She wondered what this taste in art said about their dear host. Perhaps she was fortunate not to have met Mr. Stauf yet.

But, speaking of Mr. Stauf, she had to show Edward the reason for their visit.

"Here, Edward," she said, pointing at a painting in the exact middle of the gallery. "This is what I brought you here for."

Edward turned to look at it with her.

"Ah," he said softly. "I see."

They were looking at a portrait labelled "Henry Stauf."

Except his face was made of patches of color, some flesh tone, others red and green.

"How very odd," Edward allowed.

"There's a way to change this," she said excitedly. This was something else she had discovered upon her earlier visit to this room. But she hadn't wanted to finish the puzzle alone, in case there were any—well, consequences.

She reached below the portrait of Stauf and pressed the bottom of the frame, and one of the squares changed from red to green.

"This is our puzzle. If we solve it, we'll win the prize." She ran a hand along Edward's arm. "Why don't you try it?"

Tentatively at first, then with more assurance as he deter-mined the logic of it, Edward Knox manipulated the squares in Stauf's portrait. In no time at all, they had Henry Stauf looking human.

Well, as human as he looked. Martine was happy all over again to have chosen Edward Knox as her consort.

Martine took a step away from the portrait. She won-dered what would happen next.

The frame was suddenly blank, a white field where Henry Stauf's picture had been. An instant later, the white was gone, replaced by another picture. But this time, the picture was moving, like a silent film.

Edward gasped. But Martine looked closely for clues, as if this were a puzzle within the puzzle and held the answer that would give them their reward.

The first thing that drew her attention in the picture was the boy.

The boy was being pulled through a door, into a room. He was kicking and screaming. He saw two people drag-ging him to something sitting in a chair.

"That's us," Edward whispered, pointing at the two with the boy. "My God—that's us!"

"Yes," Martine said patiently. She turned to him and smiled. "Now we know what we have to do. We have to find that boy." She pointed at the still moving painting, the boy close to the thing in the chair, the thing reaching out for the boy.

"We have to find the last guest and bring him up there."

This, then, was the final piece to the puzzle and the key to their reward.

She smiled at Edward. "Could anything be simpler?"

Edward Knox nodded. The way Martine described it, it all seemed so straightforward. Grab a boy and deliver him to a room, and their every desire would be fulfilled.

He looked over at the beautiful woman in red. He was glad Martine was so confident. It was so strange to be with a woman who knew what she really wanted. But her drive, her sense of purpose, would see both of them through. Together, they would win.

And they would have everything. Knox would leave his old life behind. He and Martine would go someplace where Whitey Chester and his men could never find them.

It was all possible. Martine smiled at him. So much was possible now.

He glanced up at the other strange portraits that filled the room; the sick, twisted paintings somehow seemed perfectly suited to this house.

A house he would leave a much richer man.

But what about his wife? What about Elinor?

He used to watch over her so carefully. Now he didn't even know if she was alive or dead.

What would happen to her? Surely Whitey and the boys wouldn't bother his wife after he was gone. Sweet, ineffectual Elinor. She was probably waiting in her room until this was all over. He would have to leave Martine for just a moment when this was all over and tell his wife that it was time to leave.

Then, of course, he would be gone. No goodbyes. It was easier that way.

Edward heard another voice. It took him a second to realize that the painting he was looking at was speaking to him.

"If you think my eyes are big," the child in the portrait said, "you should see my teeth!"

Then the child opened its mouth to show great spiked teeth, more suited to a shark than a small child.

Other pictures were talking now, too, the voices drowning each other out as they cried for attention.

Knox felt Martine grab his hand and pull him away. Thank goodness for her presence of mind.

He'd only feel good once they were rid of this place!

The voices shouted at them as they left the room, mad paintings in Stauf's madhouse. At least Martine held his hand tight. For the moment, that was enough.

He hoped she would never let go.

Julia had to admit it. Maybe she shouldn't have been quite so skeptical about some of the other's stories concerning this strange house. Because *this* was very strange.

The pot on top of the stove was bubbling away as if it still had a full fire beneath it.

Perhaps, she thought at first, someone had turned the heat back up when she was so intent upon the puzzle. But there was no flame under the kettle.

The way the stew boiled was almost violent.

There was some simple reason for all of this. She was having a bit of trouble thinking straight. All that wine, and not a bite to eat. She felt so hungry. And the soup looked so inviting, a deep, dark red broth.

She picked up the large wooden spoon she'd stirred the soup with and skimmed the surface of the broth. It was so hot, she'd have to be careful. But she really did need something in her stomach. Surely, that would settle everything right down.

Something shifted inside the pot.

Her face was sprayed by the stinging spittle of exploding bubbles. She yelled and dropped the spoon as the hot liquid stung her cheeks.

Cautiously, Julia looked over the lip of the kettle. Something had risen to the top of the pot. A large piece of meat floated on the surface of the soup.

And the meat opened a pair of eyes.

Other features followed, soup streaming from the nose and open mouth.

No. Julia wanted to run away, but she couldn't move. This couldn't be happening. It had to be the wine.

The blood-red head rose from the bubbling pot to face Julia, its eyes only a few inches from her own.

"Bring him to me." Steam issued from its lips as it spoke. Its breath smelled like death and decay.

Julia had never smelled anything so vile. She wanted to retch, to spew all the wine inside her across the kitchen floor. She had to get away from this thing, before the rot that spewed from its mouth took her, too.

"No, please no—" she gasped, "—let me—"

But the face seemed to come even closer. Her whole world was nothing but the face, shouting at her, commanding her.

"To the room at the top!" the face demanded. "Bring him to me!"

What did it mean? She couldn't understand. She had to get away.

She shook her head.

The face stared at her. And, for the first time, she looked deeply back into that gaze.

There was something there, deep inside. Something beyond the soup and the stench of decay.

Something that called to the deepest part of her. Something that knew her pain, her grief, and what she really needed.

Everything was different now. If she looked deep enough into those eyes, she would understand.

The face opened its mouth wide, as if it would take a bite out of Julia.

But then the open mouth turned into a smile.

Julia smiled back.

TWENTY-TWO

He watched it all from his tower room. The final game would play itself out at last.

They had all come, all seven of them, as he knew they would. After all, he had been reassured that everything would fall into place. And when had the voices ever been wrong?

He had helped in his way. But then, he knew so much about people's greed. And their pitiful little dreams. The first six had had no choice, really, once they had received invitations to join the richest man in town. What else could they do? Free will was really so overrated.

Of course, once the guests were inside the house, free will had ceased to exist.

And in a way, the seventh guest, the boy, was the easiest one of all. After all, Henry Stauf did have a way with children. Especially when Stauf could bribe them to see things his way, and perhaps send another one of their number—a special child—on a special dare.

He enjoyed playing so with people, especially the sort of people who used to laugh at Henry Stauf—the people who turned away when he asked for money or food, who looked down on him for spending time in jail.

Like all the people—every last one—who lived in this self-important little town.

Oh, he did have to admit there were a few who might pay attention to him, if they thought they could get something from him in return. Like that saloon keeper who put him up in that dingy back room so that he could make toys for the whiny child. He paid back that hypocritical kindness in full, when the little girl was one of the first to die. The first whining child out of the way.

One third of the children in town were out of the way now.

As far as Henry Stauf was concerned, that was a great beginning.

The parents' wails were music to his ears. Ignore Henry Stauf? Spit on him, almost drive him from town? And then, when he has something you want, like his very special toys, then fawn all over him, throw money at him. But never, ever treat him like a human being.

The good people of this town had neglected a couple of facts. Henry Stauf never forgets. And Henry Stauf always pays in full.

He knew that was why the voices had picked him, out of all the people in the world. Henry Stauf had a very special singleness of purpose. Henry Stauf never wavered; he was a bright shining light to lead the way.

Some might call him merciless, without remorse. But that was what the voices needed. He was glad to help them, after they showed him the sort of things he could do with their assistance. The voices had offered something to Henry Stauf no human had ever tried: a straight bargain, no strings attached.

And tonight, after all these months of planning and toil, the bargain would be sealed. And the seven guests in Stauf's mansion would give their lives.

That, after all, was the first part of the bargain.

But it was only after the guests died that things would get truly interesting.

TWENTY-THREE

Tad hadn't realized there was someone in the room already. He almost bolted back through the door when he saw the old man, wearing a turban and cape, sitting by a chess board. But the old man was crying.

"Hey, wha—" the old man said as he looked straight at Tad. "Who are you?

Tad hadn't wanted this to happen. He didn't belong here. He didn't want to meet anyone.

"I just want to get out of here," he found himself answering. "Please. Let me get out of here."

The man in the turban frowned at him.

"Who are you?" he demanded. "Why did you come here?"

Tad didn't know if he should answer any questions. Maybe he should get out of here, away from the crying man and all his crazy friends.

But the man hadn't threatened him or anything. Tad couldn't just run from room to room, either. He had to calm down, try to think this through. Maybe the old man knew a way out of this place.

The turbaned man smiled. Somehow, Tad found that more frightening than his anger and tears.

"Wait!" the man cried excitedly. "Wait. I do know who you are. I know who you are. You're the seventh guest. And what I just saw—"

He looked down at the chessboard in front of him, then back up at Tad.

"No," he insisted. "I understand. Oh, sweet God, I understand."

What was the old man talking about? He sounded every bit as crazy as that lady downstairs, looked as crazy as the other lady down the hall. Tad balanced on the balls of his feet, ready to run. Crazy or not, this guy was an adult; he could have a key to the front door. But Tad had to leave. How could Tad make this guy understand?

"Mister, I'm sorry," Tad blurted. "I just came in here. They dared me."

But the old man kept pointing at the chessboard, as if it was supposed to mean something. Did the guy in the turban want him to play?

"The king!" He was really shouting now. "You're the one. You!"

This was too much for Tad. This guy really was as crazy as the others. Who knew what these people would do to him?

"I'm going to leave, Mister," Tad said softly. He backed toward the door. "I'm goin' to—"

The turbaned man held his hands out toward him, as if he could somehow hold Tad back.

"No, stop!" he called after Tad. "Don't run away. You can't—"

But Tad was already gone.

Elinor couldn't stay in this bedroom. Not after what had happened.

It seemed to take all her energy to rise from the bed. As if her struggle with—what was it? Stauf, a ghost, something else, something that made you have nightmares—had drained out all her will.

But that was the evil thing's purpose. She knew that what had happened here was no more her imagination than any of her other visions. And she was determined not to let it beat her.

She pushed herself from the bed at last, using her momentum to stagger from the room.

Hamilton Temple stood in front of a door halfway down the hall. He saw her and waved. "Elinor! Come here."

Oddly, walking down the hall was far easier, far less tiring, as if, in leaving her bedroom, she had broken the spell. She was glad to comply, glad to have somebody else make the decisions for the moment. She walked quickly down the hall.

Temple's face looked different than it had before, all red and puffy. Had Temple been crying? Knowing this man could be brought to tears made her feel closer to him. She wondered if he had seen something as strange—and upsetting—as her last experience.

She thought about asking him to explain. But then she might have to explain as well. Somehow, she couldn't tell him what had happened to her. Not just yet. It felt too private, too personal. Perhaps, if Temple opened up first, and talked about what had happened to make him cry, she might feel differently. Perhaps.

By the way he was waving, he wanted to show her something. Something about the house. And it was far easier for both of them to talk about the house than about their own feelings.

Temple pointed at a closed door to his right.

"This door had been locked. I tried it when I came in." He placed his hand on the knob. "But now?"

He pushed the door open.

The room beyond was entirely filled with dolls, shelves and shelves of them.

"Dolls," Temple repeated the obvious. "Why would Stauf keep this room, a room filled with dolls, locked?"

They both stepped into the room to take a closer look. Elinor saw that every doll was different—the clothes, the hair style, the face. There were hundreds of dolls here, no two of them alike.

Each doll was an individual. That struck Elinor as an odd thought, but somehow it sounded right.

"Unless—" the magician murmured.

She looked up at Temple. All the color had drained from his face.

"Oh, God," he added softly. "I know what this is. What all these dolls are."

Elinor frowned. She didn't understand at all. She wondered if this had something to do with what had happened to Temple before.

"Don't you see?" Temple demanded. "Don't you see what this is?"

She shook her head. She didn't see at all. They were nothing but dolls—very lifelike, amazingly detailed—but only dolls.

"They're the—" Temple began as she reached out to touch the nearest doll.

But the dolls interrupted him.

"I want to be an architect," said the one Elinor had touched, a boy doll in blue jeans and a turquoise sweatshirt. The boy doll smiled.

Elinor gasped and started to pull away. But the expression on Temple's face—a mix of concentration and fascination, perhaps even delight—stopped her. There was no fear in him. Instead, he seemed almost overcome with the wonder of it all. When she looked back at the dolls, she could feel it, too. Unlike so much in Stauf's mansion, Whatever was in these dolls, there was no evil here.

Temple touched another doll in turn, a little girl doll in a pretty flowered dress.

"I love my Mommy," the second doll wailed. "Where's my Mommy?"

Elinor brought her hand to her mouth. She knew that voice. And she knew that face.

She had had a friend with a daughter, a little girl named Samantha. But Samantha had gotten sick, at the same time as all those other children. The doctors couldn't figure out what was wrong.

Samantha had died . . .

Clutching a Henry Stauf doll.

Elinor turned and looked at Temple. She almost couldn't believe what she was about to say.

"I know that voice. She lived near us. Samantha. She got sick and . . ." She looked past the magician, at row after row of tiny, perfect forms.

"Oh, God, the dolls . . ."

"Are the children," Temple finished the terrible thought for her. "The children's spirits became these dolls."

Stauf turned these children into dolls? A dozen different thoughts jumbled together in Elinor's head:

How could anyone—

It was horrible—

No one would believe such a thing—

But Elinor believed it.

As would anyone who had spent time in Henry Stauf's mansion.

"That was his deal," Temple continued, his conviction growing with every word. "Stauf took the children. Not all of them. A certain number. And—"

The dolls all started to speak, as if they had only been waiting for someone to reveal their secret.

"Take me home!"

"I want my daddy!"

"Can I play now? Can I please?"

Elinor nodded. It all made a strange kind of sense. She could feel the children—hundreds of children—all around her. Children whose lives had been taken from them, children whose spirits were trapped in these little bits of wood and cloth before her. It was all so horrible, and all so sad.

Something about this house, or Stauf's power over this house, had kept her spells—her feeling the good and bad in things—in check. But when Stauf had appeared to her, grabbing her as if he would take her soul as well, it had somehow cleared away the barriers. Her spirit sense was back, her "spells," as Edward called them, that could look inside a person or thing and show them as they truly were. She could see now, perhaps even more clearly than she had before. And she saw inside all the hundreds of dolls, each one animated by the spark of a child.

But why? She closed her eyes and let her spirit tell her.

"A certain number," she said softly. "Needed for tonight."

But there was something missing. The force that held all these children's souls still also had an empty place, a void that needed to be filled. Whatever purpose these dolls held, whatever force kept the children's spirits here, it was not finished. The spell was not complete.

Temple stared at her. "What? What was that you just said?"

"For tonight!" she replied. "These children had to be collected."

But why? She ran her hands along the row of dolls.

Give me your secrets, children, she thought.

And the children, or those spirits who once were children, answered her thoughts. Their voices spoke directly to her, inside her head.

"So dark. So dark."

"Don't let them get us!"

"They can't get us anymore, silly. We're dead."

So, Elinor thought, somehow the spirits don't only talk to me. They can talk to each other.

Somebody giggled. Somebody else broke down and cried.

"They need a child," another of the spirit voices added, "a child who is still alive."

Could she ask them questions, too? She looked up at Temple. He nodded back to her, encouraging her to go on. He seemed so much more worldly than she was. Could he guess that she might be able to communicate with the spirits of these children? At least, Elinor thought, she could try.

What do you mean? she asked them back. A child who is still alive?

"Only children give them what they need," a voice replied. "The power."

"The strength to come here," another added.

Other voices followed quickly, getting louder in her head, demanding to be heard:

"I want my mommy!"

"They can't hurt us anymore. We're dead."

"We're dead. And we're trapped."

"Help us. Help us leave here.

"Don't let them come!"

There were so many of them. They would overwhelm her.

Elinor pulled back her thoughts and looked at Temple. They had to do something, and quickly, before Stauf could go any farther with his plans. It might be the only way to save them all.

But how could she explain what the spirits in these dolls had told her? She wasn't sure she exactly understood it herself.

"There must be another child coming here," she began. "The last guest, and—"

Temple shook his head. "No. No. He's already here. I've seen him." He looked back toward the hallway. "He ran away."

The last child was here already? It was very late then, far later than Elinor had imagined. The child-sparks were very afraid.

"Away," Temple murmured, as if the last guest, the boy, might be lost forever.

He turned quickly to Elinor. "But the others will learn about the boy. What must be done. What must happen to him."

The others. Yes, Temple was talking about the other guests. Elinor knew, some, maybe all of them, would be willing to sacrifice a boy for whatever Stauf might promise them. The others. Did that include her husband as well?

"We have to find him," Temple insisted, "and get him out."

Get him out? Yes, most certainly. Elinor had gotten a sense, vague still, more emotion than image, of what Stauf was planning when he caught the seventh guest. The spell brought a feeling that dwarfed all the senses of evil and foreboding she had had about this house and its owner. It felt a little bit like the end of the world.

Behind them, the dolls were becoming frantic, screaming hysterically.

"Help me!"

"Get me out!"

Something terrible was going to happen in this house—tonight—unless someone could stop it. And now Temple wanted her to help. Could Elinor do this? Elinor, who had spent her whole life protected, hidden from the problems of the world, hidden even from herself?

The dolls' voices were growing so loud it hurt her ears. Frowning, Temple took her arm and led her from the room and into the hallway.

But she had to help, for the boy, and the spirits of the children. Or maybe just to save her own soul.

"You look upstairs, in the attic," Temple instructed. "I'll look downstairs. Move fast, before the others—"

She nodded. There was no more time for words. She followed him quickly from the room.

The dolls cried out behind them, involved in their own strange drama. Some merely repeated the sort of things they had said back when they were children. But others cried out against what was happening now. And those others were very afraid.

"Now I have you!"

"I want to be an architect."

"And so, one day—"

"I want my Mommy!"

"Give it to me!"

"No, me! Give it to—"

"Get me out!"

"Don't do that, please don't."

"Help me!"

Their voices faded as Elinor headed for the stairs leading up, and Temple moved toward the staircase leading down. All those strange, sad dolls. Children who were no longer children. And Elinor didn't know if there was anything she could do for them.

But maybe there was still one child she could save.

TWENTY-FOUR

Brian Dutton knew the voices had to come from somewhere.

As he had moved about the house, he had tapped on the walls, tugged at woodwork, listened for any hollow places beneath his feet. There had to be a hidden passageway here somewhere.

He already knew, even before he'd stumbled on that weird scene with Hamilton Temple, that this was more than just a simple game. Funny how nobody talked about the implications of Stauf's notes. To Dutton, the message was clear. Only one of the six guests would walk out of this house alive. They were playing for life and death.

Life and death. And Brian Dutton would survive them all, just as he had survived his brother all those years ago.

But the secret passages were too well hidden, at least on a first circuit of the hall and common rooms. He had decided he needed a rest. Just a few minutes; he was competing with the other five, after all. He wouldn't win anything unless he could stay reasonably sharp. So he had retreated to his room.

And a very nice room it was. That huge oriental rug alone must have cost as much as Dutton's last three business deals. And—how thoughtful—Stauf had left him a bottle of champagne!

Dutton chuckled. Now this was the way he always wanted to live! No more penny ante business deals. Real money and real luxury all the time, and all he had to do was perform one little job, one "special service" for Henry Stauf.

He just wished Stauf wasn't taking his own sweet time telling Dutton what that service was. Still, he imagined the toymaker had his reasons.

There was a briefcase on the bed, a briefcase on which had been laid a number of silver coins. Dutton thought about pocketing the coins—they looked old, they might be quite valuable—when he realized the coins, and the brief-case beneath them, were parts of another puzzle.

This whole place was full of puzzles—another of Stauf's peculiarities. This one with the coins looked like simplicity itself. The coins had different numbers on either side. Dutton found himself moving the coins about, rearranging the pattern so that it conformed with the design stamped into the briefcase, then flipping the coins over so that the coin numbers fell in the proper order.

It took surprisingly few moves, hardly a puzzle worthy of Stauf.

He heard a door open.

Dutton looked up, ready for some intruder, maybe even Stauf himself., but it wasn't the door to the hall that had swung open; it was what Dutton had assumed was the closet door, but if there had ever been a closet behind it, that space was now gone.

Instead, Dutton could see a passageway. And from that passageway came the sound of a choir.

This was the secret passageway he had been looking for all along, and the entryway was here, in Dutton's bedroom. What wonderful irony! Of course, Stauf had planned it this

way from the first. Once Dutton had solved the puzzle, the
door had opened: Stauf's reward for a job well done.
Dutton felt like the choir was singing just for him.

Dutton jumped from the bed and hurried down the passageway. The words became clearer as he approached:

> "Mystere, fara, Asteroth!
> Manitas, morto-ra
> Hala, hala, Asteroth
> *Hass! Hass!*"

The words of the choir seemed to be in some unknown
tongue, some language long dead; the choir voices, both
low and high, had a bit of an hysterical quality to them, as
if they were shouting the words as well as singing them.

The music swelled, as if the choir were calling for something to happen, or for someone to appear. An image
formed in Dutton's mind of great stone gods, fearsome
creatures fifty feet high carved into the sides of mountains. Now, why had he thought of that?

Dutton was happy, for the moment, that he didn't know
what the choir's words meant.

The choir stopped singing as he stepped into another
room.

This was a chapel, thought Dutton. The long room had
rows of benches to either side. Ornate carvings adorned
the walls. But when he looked at the carvings, they were
not the sort of things he expected, the usual saints and
crosses and ornamental fronds. Instead, he saw leering
beasts, twisted gargoyles with claw hands pressed together
in mock reverence. And yet the fantastic creatures were so
lifelike in their design that they looked ready to leap from
their perches, ready to swoop down at Dutton and tear at
him with their claws.

Dutton looked down to the other end of the room. There, at the top of a short flight of stone steps, was an altar, a table covered with a wine-red cloth.

Dutton took a step into the room.

An intense stabbing sensation brought him to his knees. Dutton clutched at his side.

"Oh God," he whispered. "The pain." Somehow, he managed to step back to where he had entered the room.

And the pain was gone.

Dutton looked back to where he had just walked, and where he had just felt like he was going to die. He couldn't see any reason for such a sudden pain, no sharp objects or wires. And there were no marks on his shirt where he had felt the stabbing—even though that feeling had been very real.

This was another of Stauf's tricks. Dutton looked back across the room. He felt that Stauf wanted him to reach that altar; that was the reason Dutton, and only Dutton, had been privileged to hear the choir. There was something about that altar, or something on that altar, that must be the special service that Stauf had mentioned in his letter, the service that only Dutton could perform.

But if Stauf wanted to bring Dutton to the altar, why did he give Dutton such pain when he tried to approach it?

It was another puzzle, Dutton realized, another test. Before Dutton could achieve his heart's desire, he had to prove himself worthy.

But this was different from the earlier puzzles, the earlier tests. A misstep in this puzzle would bring Dutton agony. No doubt if he stepped the wrong way more than once, the agony would increase.

Failure at this puzzle, Dutton realized, might end in death.

But this whole house reeked of death. Dutton could turn back, leave the chapel and this difficult game, and die anyway. Or he could go forward and win everything he had ever wanted.

So solve the puzzle, Dutton told himself, or you die.

He looked down at the floor. Something had hurt him—why? The stones that made up the floor were a multi-colored jumble, the color of a harlequin's outfit.

The pain was telling him something. There's a rule to walking on these stones.

He took a step. Nothing. He had guessed correctly. The first stone had been red, the same color as the altar cloth. Perhaps the red stones were the safe path across the room.

But the second step brought more pain than before, a stabbing sensation deep in his intestines, as if someone was using a knife on Dutton's insides.

The leering gargoyles swam in his dizzy vision, as if they were waiting for him to fall so that they might rip him apart. Shadows rippled across the stones, as if the floor might give way to a yawning pit and plunge him to his death.

He looked up and saw another stained glass window, appropriate even in this chapel. And that window held all the colors of the rainbow.

That, Dutton realized, could be the answer.

The first stone he had stepped on was red. When he had stepped on another red stone, it had brought him pain. He was supposed to step on one red, and no more.

The floor tiles contained all the colors of the rainbow, too. And he had to follow the rainbow to the altar.

Red was first, next orange.

No pain.

Yellow, then green.

Still nothing.

Blue. A leap to indigo. Then violet.

He looked up and saw that, somehow, in those few short steps, he had crossed the room to the altar. His fingers reached out and touched the cloth.

The cloth began to rise without any help from Dutton.

The candlelight in the temple flickered.

And Dutton saw something not quite real, but something that showed him the true purpose of this room—perhaps what had happened in this chapel of the damned, over and over again, since the day this house was built.

He saw Stauf dressed in a crimson robe, laughing like some mad priest. He held a naked infant in his hands; but the child seemed even less real than Stauf, fading in and out of view as Dutton watched, as if it were the ghost of a child.

What did this vision mean? Did Stauf control the ghosts of children? It would not surprise Dutton in the least if this house were full of ghosts; he was surprised, really, how readily he accepted such a thought.

But then, things were different inside Stauf's mansion. He had been here only a matter of hours, and already Dutton might be willing to accept anything. He could feel the spirits now, hundreds of them, as if all he had to do was acknowledge their existence for them to show themselves. They flew about the chapel, about the whole house, in a big, noisy jumble, fueled by the energy of the young, as if they could not quite admit they were dead. But as much as they flew and bounced about this place, they were trapped. Stauf had made sure there was no way out for the ghosts.

Just as he made sure there was no way out for his seven guests. No, Dutton reminded himself. That was only true for six of the guests. He was the exception. Brian Dutton had trained himself to be a survivor. He would be the lucky one.

Were these ghosts—the spirits of children—the source of Stauf's power? Dutton felt they had something to do with it, but there was more to it than that.

For Dutton could sense something else in this room, something hanging near the altar, something that he couldn't quite see, but that was there nonetheless, like a mist just before dawn. Dutton guessed it was some other spirit form, something that lived more easily in Stauf's mansion than it would in the outside world.

What could it be? Dutton almost laughed. He had suddenly seen the ghosts, and now he expected to have all the answers right in front of him.

He moved closer to this "other"; Dutton didn't know what else to call it. Whether it was one great thing or many smaller ones, Dutton wasn't sure. He reached a hand forward to touch them—and felt a sensation beyond cold, beyond darkness, beyond pain.

He looked down at his hand and was surprised to see it was still whole.

He realized he had pulled his hand away as soon as contact was made, like backing away from fire.

The things had barely brushed at his flesh. But even with the slightest contact he could feel how much they wanted his warmth, how much they wanted his life.

These were things that did not belong in this world, at least not the world that Brian Dutton knew. But Stauf had brought them here, and they gave Stauf power. They were so close to this world, now, like whispers that you couldn't quite hear, but they were whispers demanding to become shouts.

These whispers had never seen this world, but they wanted to. Dutton could feel their desire. And Stauf was helping them. He was using the children to do that. And maybe Stauf was left with nothing but ghosts because he had fed these things the children's lives.

Stauf gained power with the lives of children?

Dutton shook his head. He was beyond judgment.

Brian Dutton had left his own brother behind, a child drowning beneath the ice. That was the end of his feelings about children, and family, and anything else except what was best for Brian Dutton. Stauf could do whatever he wanted to, to whomever he wanted, as long as Brian Dutton won. Dutton could look at a hundred children trapped beneath the ice while he counted his money. Brian Dutton would be the lucky one.

The image of Stauf suddenly spoke. Dutton had almost forgotten he was there. But Stauf's words were soft, distorted. Dutton could make no sense of them.

Stauf muttered to the twisting ghost of one child, a captured spirit.

The shapes moved closer. Dutton thought he saw them, even though they were only halfway here, pulsating with energy. These were the source of Stauf's power, and they would give power to Dutton as well. The patterns they made were hypnotizing; he felt himself drawn towards the cold, drawn towards the pain. He had to look away.

Dutton shook his head.

The image of Stauf looked straight at him. The toymaker, wrapped in a red cloth, master of this black mass for things from the beyond, spoke at last in words Dutton could understand.

"Now," Stauf commanded. "Now the sacrifice must come from you. It must be brought to me—alive. A final sacrifice."

For an instant, the child on the altar changed, growing from a baby to a young man just short of adolescence. And Dutton realized that this was his special service, to find this child and bring him to Stauf. A final sacrifice, a final piece to the bargain made by Stauf with these whispers.

Dutton hesitated.

What would happen when these things were let loose in this world—these things that fed on children, these things that fed on life?

Then Dutton saw his reward. It was just a brief image, but it was wonderful. He saw a great house and people to take his orders, to fulfill his every command. No more shabby offices, no more business deals, no more back-stabbing.

And no more worrying if he was better than his brother. No one could want more than this.

The whispers wouldn't bother him. Dutton would be the lucky one. Dutton would be better than everybody.

With that, the vision was gone. Dutton looked up to see Stauf smiling down at him. And the ghost Stauf offered

Dutton the knife in his hand. A ghost knife, thought Dutton. Another illusion.

Still, Dutton reached forward, and his hand closed around the blade. To his surprise, his fingers brushed something cold and solid. A shock went through him, as if the knife held some part of Stauf's great power, the power from the beyond. Then the energy faded, and Dutton felt the cold metal in his hand. The knife was real.

Stauf, and the things he served, needed a real sacrifice to complete their ascension; they needed the blood of a boy, a boy who was already in this house, only a few feet away.

Dutton had a job to do, his "special service." The knife was only a tool, the murder only an unpleasant bit of business. Dutton was a businessman, after all. And then, when it was done, he would get the only thing that truly mattered—his reward.

Stauf wheeled himself from the shadows once Dutton was gone. Of all the rooms in the house, this was his favorite. This chapel was where his power truly began.

He did not want to show himself to the others until the proper time. Someone might think he had aged twenty years in a dozen months, but appearance was deceiving. He was stronger than anyone.

And it was all going so well. Everyone—all his guests— were fitting in so well with his plans. Oh, there were a few surprises, but nothing that he, and the powers that guided him, couldn't handle with the greatest of ease.

He rested his hand on the altar, an altar drenched through with blood, and perhaps with children's souls.

He could hear the children's voices, even now, the little pieces of their souls still left trapped in the dolls. Crying out for parents and playmates and all the parts of their lives that had been snatched away.

Those other voices, the ones that had guided his hand since he had picked up that first hammer to crush that first skull, those voices had asked so much of him. But he had given them what they needed.

Stauf thought he heard the doll-children grow angry, as if they wanted to reach out from their wooden prisons to overwhelm him. Stauf knew what still lived in those dolls hated him. They would destroy him if they could. But the other voices had reserved him for a greater purpose.

He felt the power enter him again through his hands, filling him with a joy and sense of purpose. It didn't matter what he had to do. When the voices filled him this way, anything was worth it.

The voices sang to him. He opened his own mouth to shout along, drowning out the distant voices of the children. The power lifted his chair from the stone floor and spun him about, turning him toward his destination. It was time for that one final act that would seal the bargain forever.

With the voices inside him, Stauf was unstoppable.

Tad ran downstairs instead. He didn't want to hide. He wanted out, away from all these crazy people.

He ran all the way to the front door, hoping somehow that it would be unlocked, that there was some way to get it open.

He jiggled the handle, talked to it, begged it to open. "Come on, come on—"

It didn't budge.

There was no way out of the crazy house.

There are people, his mother had told him, people who do bad things to kids. They catch kids, and then they do bad things to them.

Tad's Mom never told him what those things were. She just looked at him in that way she had, narrowing her eyes to slits, and he could imagine.

Bad things. In the crazy house.

"Please!" he cried. He didn't see a lock on the door, no latch to turn, nothing to make the knob work. "Please, come on!"

Something in the kitchen howled. Tad wasn't even sure if the noise was human.

Tad ran the opposite direction.

The first room he looked into held a piano and a whole bunch of plants. Farther up the hall, through an open door, he could see another room filled with books. That was the room where all the others had had a meeting before, the only room Tad hadn't explored. Maybe there was an open window in there, or a door to the outside.

The piano started to play. It was a tune he remembered his mother singing a long time ago, a lullaby. Back when his mother used to sing him to sleep, back before she just ordered him to go to bed.

Tad stopped and stared. The piano played all by itself. Tad had seen one of these funny pianos once before, when his family had gone on vacation in the mountains. A player piano, that's what they called it.

But then he saw movement above the keys. A pair of hands, nothing but hands, the fingers hitting the keys, the hands playing the piano.

He backed away.

And other hands grabbed him from behind.

TWENTY-FIVE

Now the players had received given their tools, and the final drama would begin.

Henry Stauf sat back in his chair and smiled.

As impatient as he had been, he wanted to savor the moment for just a little while.

He had so few moments like this.

Of course, life had taken a turn for the better when the voices came to him. Stauf no longer had to live under other people's rules, or try somehow to live up to their expectations. Instead, he made up his own rules, in the shape of toys and games and puzzles.

Who needed the approval of a father, or a wife, or even the town constable? How much simpler life was when you could play games. When you could solve puzzles.

Games and puzzles had beginnings and ends. Games and puzzles could be controlled. Except that, sometimes, the ending was a surprise.

There were far fewer surprises when you created all the games yourself.

Stauf, guided by the voices, had a talent for invention, and a gift for creating things that spoke to children's souls.

The children were only the beginning.

Those pitiful, whining children. It was so easy to win their trust. So simple to give them—and make them want—the instruments of their own destruction.

All to feed the voices. And the voices gave to Henry Stauf in turn.

Now it was time for the final act. To set six of those fine citizens of this town at each other's throats—the staid Knoxes, the kind of couple who would never look at a homeless Henry Stauf; the beautiful Martine Burden, too lovely, too full of herself to even consider a balding man who lived in the gutter; the cut-throat businessman Brian Dutton, who would be glad to exploit anyone as long as he could walk over them later; and the once great Hamilton Temple, who actually thought he knew a thing or two about magic.

Stauf chuckled. It was going to be such fun to watch them fall.

And what about his other invited guest? He had a very special place for old, self-centered, alcoholic Julia Heine. After all, she so reminded Stauf of his mother.

And then there was the last visitor to the house, the seventh guest: Tad Gorman, a child, so innocent, so easily manipulated. Blameless, really. Stauf laughed out loud. His destruction would be the sweetest of all.

For the child's blood would open the way.

Stauf could barely contain his excitement.

The voices would fulfill their promise at last. And Stauf would let the voices have the world.

See what happens, people? See what happens when you treat Henry Stauf this way? You never cared about me!

And he never cared about any of them. Others never understood. He didn't have to play by their rules.

Henry Stauf was preparing for the final act. He would have what was his at last.

For the first time ever, Henry Stauf was happy.

And that was very bad news for the rest of the world.

He would make all of them pay.

TWENTY-SIX

Now Dutton had him. The seventh guest, all ready to be served up on a platter to their host. In exchange, Henry Stauf would give Brian Dutton what he truly desired.

Dutton pulled the kid close, and the boy started kicking right away. Like the kid knew what was happening, like this was life and death.

Because that's just what it was. Death for the kid, the best of lives for Brian Dutton.

Dutton yanked his captive back and forth a couple times to wear him out. Dutton had to hold the kid too close to really give him a good slug, the kind of thing that would shock the kid and quiet him down. Plus Dutton had to be careful here. He didn't want to damage the merchandise. One small accident, and Dutton could lose everything. Stauf wanted the child alive.

The kid just wouldn't stop struggling. This was getting tiresome. Dutton had already gone halfway to Hell to get what he wanted. And here he was with another trial on his hands. Dutton thought about the knife he had hidden beneath his jacket. He decided that, right now, it was too risky. The kid was damn lucky Stauf wanted him in one piece.

Still, the kid didn't need to know that. Dutton leaned close to the kid's ear and whispered.

"Stop struggling. Stop it, or I'll squeeze you 'til you pop."

That slowed the kid down a little. Dutton grinned. A little fear could do wonders.

Behind them, the piano kept on playing, a livelier music now than the sleepy music it had played before, as if it wanted Dutton and the boy to dance a jig.

Next door in the library, the glass doors blew open with a crash. Dutton heard the rustling of the leaves and rain falling on the cement patio. Perhaps the house could no longer contain all the excitement, and had thrown open its doors so that it wouldn't burst. The end—the glorious end—was very close, only a couple of flights of stairs away.

The end of everybody else, that is, and the beginning of Dutton's reward. But he had a job to finish first.

He had to bring the boy up, all the way up. Up to the room at the top of the house, the pinnacle of this glorious, crazy mansion. The room where Stauf had waited all along.

Dutton started to pull the boy back towards the hallway and the stairs.

He turned around to find the doorway, the struggling boy still clutched to his chest. This was going to be a little awkward, but Dutton would find a way. His brother was the one who died. Brian Dutton was the survivor.

The door was directly ahead of them. Dutton took his first step towards his great reward.

And Edward Knox and Martine Burden walked into the room.

Tad's mouth was covered by the man's hand. Tad tried to struggle, to bite the hand that covered his mouth. But the man's grip was much too firm, his hand clamped too tightly on Tad's jaw. Tad couldn't move his mouth at all.

The man had gripped Tad's right arm, too, adult fingers digging painfully into boy's muscles. And every time Tad tried to struggle, the man's grip got tighter.

But Tad could still see.

Two other people came into the room. A pretty young woman, maybe in her twenties, and a thin man a few years older than his father. The woman smiled and touched this other man on the arm, as if the two of them shared a joke, or a secret. The thin man looked like he didn't want to be here.

Maybe they can stop the guy who grabbed me, Tad thought. Maybe they'll save me. Maybe everybody isn't crazy here.

Instead, the two newcomers stared at Tad, as if he were the secret they had been talking about. The secret, or the joke.

"He's ours, Dutton," the thin and nervous man said. "We figured out what to do. He's ours—"

Tad craned his head around to try and see the man holding him, the one named Dutton. But Dutton's grip was still too tight.

"No," Dutton said. "I got the boy. I won. I figured out the puzzle."

They were fighting over him. Like he was some sort of prize. For what? Tad didn't want to think about it. One thing was for sure: None of these three people had even thought about asking what Tad wanted.

Tad's mother's words about bad people and bad things filled his head. He felt an involuntary shiver.

Then the woman touched the man again. Tad had seen kids do that sort of thing at school, pushing another kid to do something that he didn't really want to do.

Like the way Billy Dumphy and all the other kids had pushed Tad to come into this house. Would the thin and nervous man be as stupid as Tad?

The thin man took a step towards Dutton.

"We'll take him." The thin man was trying to sound tough, but Tad thought it sounded all wrong, like he wasn't used to acting this way. "Up to the attic. Up to Henry Stauf and our reward."

The thin man took another step towards them. He looked like he was trying to get his nerve up, like kids do before a fight.

Dutton's hand released Tad's arm. Tad could feel Dutton shift his weight behind him.

Silver flashed to Tad's right. He tried to yank away from the hand that still held his jaw, to twist around and get a better look.

Dutton's grip gave slightly before his hand clamped down again, and Tad could see the silver thing by his ear.

Dutton had drawn a knife.

But all of Dutton's attention was on the man and woman across the room, and Dutton was holding Tad with only one hand. If Tad could just twist away from the knife, maybe he could break free.

"Give us the boy, Dutton," the thin man insisted. "We know what to do with him."

"Screw yourself," Dutton answered.

Tad guessed that was the wrong answer. The other man pulled his lips back from his teeth. He yelled and charged wildly, straight for Dutton.

The hand sprang away from Tad's mouth. Tad fell to the floor. But he was free!

The thin man ran straight into Dutton, jarring his arm. The knife fell to the floor. Tad rolled away from the fight. Maybe, if everybody else was fighting, he could scramble to his feet and head for the door. For the moment, though, he'd keep close to the ground and out of the way until he saw his chance.

The piano kept on playing, faster than ever, as if they were all in one of the movies Tad sometimes saw on Saturday afternoons. It sounded like the background music to some barroom brawl.

The woman dodged around the struggling men. She knelt down and grabbed the knife. She called out one word:

"Edward!"

The thin man looked around and freed up one of his hands long enough to grab the knife from the woman's hand. But the two men had stumbled between the woman and Tad. That left a clear line between Tad and the doorway to the hall. Tad took one step in that direction, then another, trying to act casual, afraid that if he moved too quickly too soon they would all try to stop him.

Tad heard a sudden grunt of pain. He saw the knife cut through Dutton's shirt and slide between his ribs. The other man, Edward, pulled it out, the silver metal now covered with deep, dark red.

Dutton made a noise deep down in his throat, half moan, half laugh, as he saw his blood on the knife.

Edward stabbed Dutton again.

The piano played faster and faster as the side of Dutton's shirt turned to reddish-brown.

Tad glanced behind him. The woman walked quickly around the struggling pair, her hands outstretched towards Tad.

"Come here, you—" she began.

But Tad was on his feet, running.

He ran from the room. But where could he go? Not upstairs. They had wanted to take him upstairs. There must be something bad there. Bad things done by bad people. Something he had to stay away from.

They had said something, too, about old man Stauf. He was up there, then, waiting for him. Waiting to do something bad. Tad remembered the rhyme all the kids had sung outside the mansion.

"Blood inside the Library,
Blood right down the hall,

Blood going up the attic stairs
Where the last guest did fall."

And the bit about Stauf, "crazy, sick, and mean." Tad believed every word of it.

Tad ran down the hall, trying to think of everything he'd seen in the other rooms. He remembered then: when he was hiding in the kitchen, he had seen stairs going down. Everything he'd tried on the first floor was all locked up. But maybe he could find a way out through the basement.

He ran down the hall and darted into the kitchen, hoping he could make it out of sight before anybody realized where he was going.

TWENTY-SEVEN

amilton Temple had been looking for the boy.

Instead, he'd found this.

A doorway had opened up on the side of the stairs between the first and second floors. At least that's what he had guessed had happened. Actually, one moment he had been hurrying downstairs, the next he had half-run, half-stumbled into this room.

Temple knew he hadn't reached this place by a totally normal route. Which, he supposed, was in keeping with the house and the evening. According to Elinor Knox, something was supposed to happen this night; that was why they were all here, to participate in that event. And, Temple guessed, the closer they came to that event, the less the rules of the real world applied.

So, maybe in this magic house, you could make magic leaps. Temple could think of no other reason for his appearance in this room.

But, if he had stumbled upon this room, others might have as well. He would have to be careful. Stauf was raising the stakes here, pitting one guest against another. Soon, whatever trappings of civility the guests had shown toward each other could be gone, lost in the mad scramble for the promised prize. After all, as Stauf had stated in Temple's letter, and no doubt the other notes as well, the prize could go to only one.

So Stauf's contest was really about survival—with extra points for ruthlessness, no doubt. And which of the guests would survive?

Temple didn't trust Brian Dutton or Martine Burden in the least; he thought that either one of them might go to any length to get what they desired. Edward Knox was self-important, but he was weak. He didn't seem like a danger by himself, but he could easily be manipulated by others. Elinor Knox, on the other hand, seemed to have a good heart. She was the one person among all the guests that Temple thought could be trusted, the one other who might be counted on to fight back against Stauf.

That left Julia Heine, who seemed to spend all her time trying to leave herself—by drinking herself into a perpetual stupor. Temple didn't think Miss Heine was as much of an immediate threat as some of the others, although, in a house like this, even she could stumble upon something that might make her dangerous.

Temple would have to look out for all of them now. And, if possible, he had to keep any and all of them, save Elinor, from getting the boy.

But who else might be here? This room he had stumbled into looked like some sort of laboratory. It did not appear to be all that large. Still, looks were often deceiving in this place.

"Boy?" he called.

He looked carefully around him, in case anyone else was hiding in the shadows.

Scientific equipment filled this place. The tables and shelves here were covered with vials, specimen jars, and arcane looking instruments. Larger containers hung from the ceiling, filled with some dark red liquid which Temple sincerely hoped wasn't blood. And the far end of the room was completely dominated by a huge machine topped off with a pair of electric coils. Temple had no idea what Stauf might use something like that for. It all looked like something out of *Dr. Jekyll and Mr. Hyde* or *Metropolis*.

Basically, Stauf had assembled a very thorough research facility. But research into what?

And yet, a room like this might hold some answers, if Temple could begin to comprehend any of the clutter.

He heard no other movement in the room. "Boy?" he called again. A large glass door appeared to lead into some sort of refrigerated compartment. Temple tried the handle, but the door was locked. Hopefully, the boy would have enough sense not to hide in a place like that anyway. He might end up frozen.

Temple was both fascinated and disappointed by this place. He had a feeling that this was where Stauf devised many of the tricks that littered the house, created by science rather than some advanced magic. They might have looked supernatural, but their causes were probably all too real.

"This," he murmured as he ran his hands along the surfaces of some of the more bizarre devices. "Yes. This is it. Not magic, but some demented—"

Did he dare call it science? It looked as though Stauf had delved into whole new realms of the arcane. Perhaps there might be a bit of magic here after all.

Sparks flew between a pair of coils against the wall. So some of these machines were working now. These might be the very machines creating the effects in the house. It would not be so difficult to come up with scientific explanations for most of them. Maybe there were hidden tape recorders, supplying all those voices for the dolls.

Of course, Elinor Knox had thought there was something deeper involved with those dolls, something Temple had been very willing to believe at the time. But supernatural events are so very difficult to prove—or disprove. That blurring of the lines between the possible and impossible was one of the cornerstones of a good magic act. And Stauf had devised a magic act of staggering complexity.

Part of Temple couldn't help admiring the sheer perverse energy that had gone into creating all of this. Stauf was truly crazy; every moment Temple spent in this house convinced him more fully of that. But his madness seemed to encompass some wild purpose that Temple could not even begin to fathom.

Temple still hoped there was some real magic behind it all.

This room must hold some hints as to how Stauf worked everything in the house. Perhaps he'd even find out where the toymaker had hidden himself. Temple wouldn't mind discovering something as simple as how to unlock the front door.

He picked up a small book from the central table. It appeared to be a diary of some sort.

"I have this day," Temple read aloud, "discovered a way to communicate with my voices."

His . . . voices? What did that mean? Was someone else feeding him all this information?

Temple flipped through the pages, skimming the cramped writing, as Henry Stauf wrote proudly about the woman he had killed, a crime for which he had never been caught, the event that led somehow, at least within Stauf's twisted brain, to the creation of the first of his dolls.

According to Stauf, his voices were from another world, perhaps even another plane of existence. They contained great power, but demanded great sacrifice.

Specifically the sacrifice of children.

But the voices were no longer satisfied with the sacrifices Stauf could provide them. They wished to enter this world, so that they might claim their own victims.

According to the book in Temple's hands, Stauf had promised to open the way for these beings, with a final sacrifice. Tonight. The way would be opened by the death of the other older guests and then, when the time was right, the blood of the child.

"I wanted power, real magic. If it existed. That's why I came here. But not this—" Temple couldn't read any farther.

He looked up to see a ghost spread on the table before him, the ghost of a man, with a hole at the top of his head. The man leaned over the edge of the table and retrieved a brain from a large bucket.

It appeared as a small tableau, performed for his benefit. A distraction, to keep him here, to prevent him from interfering with Stauf's plans.

Well, it would not work. Temple threw the book back down on the table. It passed through the ghost, and the ghost disappeared.

Temple was old, and he was tired, but he would fight Henry Stauf, and the evil he wanted to bring to this world, with every ounce of strength left in his being.

He might find answers here, but he would be lulled into forgetting all about the boy.

He would not let Stauf win.

He had one final job to do. Collect the boy and Elinor Knox and get the three of them out of there.

He might come back at some other time to learn these secrets, but not when others' lives were at stake.

Perhaps Stauf even kept himself alive with the blood of children. There were some things Temple would not pursue.

He rushed back the way he had come.

Somewhere, below him, he heard the cries of a frightened child.

Martine Burden couldn't believe this. The kid had managed to run out of the room.

Dutton had fallen to his knees, blood pouring from his wound. And Edward Knox was staring down at the knife in his hand like some big, dumb ox, as if he had never seen blood before.

"Edward!" Martine called to him. "The child! He's getting away!"

Knox's head jerked around to look at her, as if he were surprised that she was still in the room with him.

"You had to do it!" Martine insisted, walking quickly over to take his arm. "Or he would have done it to us!"

He could do nothing but stare: at Martine, at the fallen Dutton, at the knife in his hands. She marched to Knox's side, wrapped her arm around a dry portion of his sleeve, and led him from the room.

Poor Edward really was a mess. His hands and upper arms were covered with blood. She wasn't even perspiring.

Martine liked the way this was going. From now on, men would do all her dirty work.

She had seen the child run down the hallway. She turned to follow him and saw him turn quickly into the kitchen.

"This way," she urged Knox. "Quickly. We don't want to lose him."

Dutton moaned behind them. He had only gotten what he deserved. She was glad to be rid of him. Dutton could have been a problem. Not like her dear, sweet Edward.

Knox walked by her side, keeping up with her rapid pace, but not really looking where they were going. As if a simple altercation involving a knife had taken away his ability to think. That was all right with Martine, so long as, when she told him to, he would use the knife again.

The child was nowhere in the kitchen. Where could he have gone?

Martine saw the stairs leading down to the basement. And they knew, thanks to dear sweet Elinor, that there was no way out down there.

"We've got the little bastard trapped!" She tugged at Knox to lead the way down the narrow steps. "Hurry, Edward!"

Knox took the steps down so rapidly she was afraid he might fall. He started huffing and puffing as he climbed down the stairs. The poor dear would have a heart attack.

Even that was fine with Martine, so long as he got her the boy first.

Yes, this using people, letting them do all the dirty work, was another lesson well learned, one more thing she'd need to thank Mr. Stauf for. As soon as they'd delivered the boy and received their reward.

And what if Stauf wouldn't give the prize to both of them? What if he insisted on following the exact wording of the note? What if only one of the guests could remain alive?

Well, then, Martine would have to get her hands dirty after all.

TWENTY-EIGHT

Elinor heard the sounds of a struggle downstairs.
She wondered if she should turn around; go down and see if she could somehow help. What if the scuffle involved Temple or the boy?

But she had a job to do; one she and Temple had agreed upon. She had gotten the impression that Hamilton Temple could take care of himself. And that noise coming from downstairs could very likely be another of Henry Stauf's tricks, like the dripping blood in the basement that wasn't blood at all. Stauf might be trying to turn her away from the one place he was most afraid of her going.

He wanted the guests to bring him the boy. And he waited, somewhere at the very top of the stairs. But what if someone climbed those stairs without the boy? What if someone were able to stop the boy before he reached the toymaker, either by finding where the boy hid, or by stopping whoever brought the boy to Stauf?

What would happen then? Elinor hoped she would have the chance to find out.

One way or another, she was climbing up these stairs to act as a sentry, to make sure Stauf would not get what he wanted most.

Could Elinor do such a thing? Somehow, in these last few years of her marriage, she had stopped being a very active person. She had spent most of her time at home, becoming so dependent on Edward for so many things. But she had not always been married to Edward, and his job, and their sad little house and all their never-ending debts. Once, long ago, she had been an independent woman. And she would have to be independent once again.

She could certainly try to find the child. But what if someone else found him first? What if someone dragged the young man, kicking and screaming, up the stairs?

She so hoped the one who brought him up the stairs wouldn't be Edward.

Did she know her husband at all anymore?

She remembered when they had first gotten the invitation from Stauf. It felt like so much longer than just a few days. But then their time in this house felt like so much more than just a few hours. She sighed. Could one night be a lifetime? It felt like that in here.

She had had a bad feeling from the moment she had touched that invitation. But Edward had insisted that she come. And then Edward, her husband and protector, had abandoned her to a house full of dangers.

And what if Edward came up the stairs with that woman, that Martine? Perhaps Edward thought he had hidden his desire for that young woman away when all the guests had first gathered together.

But then his attitude towards his wife had changed as well. He had seemed so angry with Elinor after that incident in the basement, as if she were nothing but a bother. He had no use for his wife anymore.

She had not been at all surprised when he vanished. She had watched him ogle younger woman for a long time now, years, really, now that she thought of it. She guessed she had expected him to stray the first time one of them looked back. In that, at least, Elinor wasn't disappointed.

She still hoped Edward wouldn't bring the child.

She could certainly stop Martine, that shameless hussy. And she might be strong enough to confront Edward, but would he even admit that he had done anything wrong? Could she even begin to be strong enough to stop the two of them together?

Maybe it wouldn't come to that.

She started up the stairs.

There was another ending to this, too. She realized she might never see Edward again.

Somehow, that didn't seem anywhere near as important as it would have a few short hours ago.

Elinor had to admit it. It might have taken years to happen, but she was angry: at her hypocritical husband, at that floozy in the red dress, Martine Burden, and at that crazy toymaker who'd brought them all here, Henry Stauf.

And, Elinor admitted, she was angry at herself. She was sick and tired of letting others have power over her life. She would take power over her own life now.

She had to do this, whatever she could do, for herself.

Elinor thought she heard a new sound—soft, high voices that whispered things she couldn't quite catch. Was this another of Stauf's tricks? If it was, she had no time for it.

She stepped onto the third floor. It was a mess up here, half-workshop, half attic. Discarded toys littered the place: dolls without arms, half-carved horses, wooden blocks painted with strange symbols. Stauf's rejects, Elinor thought. The place was so crowded, it would make an excellent place to hide.

If the boy was up here, how could she get him to show himself? She wished she knew the boy's name. Could she get the boy to trust her? She didn't believe she looked very frightening. But there were many strange and dangerous things in this place, things that weren't always what they seemed. If she were the same age as the boy, she wasn't sure she would trust a soul.

What was that?

She felt it as soon as she walked away from the stairs.

She was not alone here.

She had never felt such raw power. Something permeated the air here, something evil. Did it come from Stauf? He would be very close now, this far up in the house. But somehow, she felt this power did not come from humans, or even from this world.

Somehow, she felt this power might control Stauf rather than the other way around.

She wanted to run away, to get away from this force. But she had run away for far too long. She had to face this, even if it destroyed her. Because she would be nothing if she didn't, her whole, newfound independence nothing but a sham.

She started to pick her way through the piles of toys, some only half built, the others half destroyed.

"Is anyone here?" she called.

She thought she heard some faint reply, like distant whispers from the deepest shadows; those same, childlike voices again. But she heard no shifting of debris, and none of the heavy breathing that would come from a boy on the run. He probably wasn't here. But something else was. And Elinor would find it.

Was it one of the others? She thought about all of them, considering each of them—for the first time, she realized—as individuals.

Why the six guests? Why, out of all the people in town, had Stauf picked the six of them?

She thought about the others, the tramp Martine Burden, the fading Julia Heine, the arthritic Hamilton Temple, the cut-throat Brian Dutton, and what they had in common with her husband and herself. They all, in one way or another, had wasted their lives; they had all let their dreams run away from them.

That was what Henry Stauf was offering them. Their own, slightly used dreams. But it seemed such an empty promise now.

Really, she felt that Stauf only gave lip-service to fulfilling people's dreams. The toymaker seemed much more interested in playing with them. Stauf only cared that he got what he wanted.

And what did Elinor Knox want?

She was a changed woman.

She didn't feel so important anymore. She didn't care that much about herself, or Edward, or their tarnished dreams. She was in this house for one purpose. She wanted to save the child. And, after him, maybe all the other children, too, freeing their spirits from this cursed mansion.

She heard the whispering again. But it was clearer now, clear enough for her to make out words and phrases.

"Take me home—want my mommy—Can I play now?"

The child-voices grew stronger with every word. She knew where they came from, now. Somehow, the dolls were talking to her again.

"Where are you?" she called. She thought about those other things she felt, evil things, "Are you in danger?"

"They can't hurt us anymore. We're dead."

"We're dead. And we're trapped."

"Help us. Help us leave here."

"Don't let them come!"

The doll's voices had said these same things before. But now they were making a new and horrible sense. The evil that she felt was very close. It was even more important that she find the boy.

She started to pick her way through a second pile. It looked as if there might be bits of every toy imaginable heaped in this debris. But, so far, she had found nothing living.

She had to stop and rest for a moment. Despite the urgency in the doll's voices, this place was making her very tired.

Unless, it wasn't her.

Something else was wrong with this place; a power that seemed to drain the energy from the air around her.

This power seemed to make it difficult to move, as if Stauf controlled the very air in this dusty attic. Her legs and arms moved more slowly with each pile of debris she explored.

Her joints seemed to stiffen. She was finding it difficult to move at all, as if gravity were heavier here.

Perhaps it was she who was changing. Was Stauf making her older? Perhaps she withered with every step. Perhaps, in walking from one pile of toys to the next, she would turn to dust.

She moved to brush away a strand of hair. But her fingers would not open. They seemed stuck in place.

She lifted her arm.

Her hand appeared to be made of wood.

She was no longer human. She was turning into one of Stauf's creations, a giant life-sized toy, a puppet for the toymaker to play with.

"No!"

She fell with a clatter to the attic floor.

Her voice still worked, but she could no longer feel or move her arms and legs.

"Help us!" the dolls cried again. "Don't let them come!"

Elinor began to cry. How could she help any of them when she was turning into a doll herself? This would happen to all of them. Stauf was just too strong.

If he could do this to them, how could they possibly save the boy?

Twenty-Nine

Tad hoped he hadn't made a mistake. He had rushed down the stairs without thinking, just wanting to get away from these crazy people in this crazy house.

But there was so little light down here, in this cellar, in this maze. It was hard to run here. You could trip over something, or get turned around the way the passageways twisted back and forth.

But there had to be places to hide, Tad thought. Lots of places to hide with all these twists and turns. Somewhere down here, there had to be a window or two. And a window could be opened, or glass could be smashed. There might even be a cellar door. He was pretty skinny; he could squeeze out of a small space. He'd squeezed through the kitchen window when he got into this place.

Even if the windows were tiny, maybe he could at least find a way to yell to his friends. They couldn't have all gone away. He was sure they were waiting outside, some of them at least, laughing and chewing gum, waiting to razz Tad when he came back out again. His friends wouldn't leave, no matter how late it got. Would they?

He ran down one tunnel, took a sharp right turn, ran up another.

He saw great red splotches on the ceiling, dripping down towards him. It looked like blood, drenching him in red. But he didn't stop. It was another trick, like that piano upstairs. This house was full of tricks. But Tad wasn't going to fall for them anymore.

He ran until he came to the entrance of a larger room. The room was as big as the auditorium at school, and the whole place was filled with boxes. They were long boxes, too, boxes that looked like coffins.

But boxes or coffins, they couldn't keep still. Their lids seemed to be constantly moving, up and down, in and out, like some giant puzzle.

That's what this place was, all tricks and puzzles. He stood there for a long moment, watching the coffin lids slam open and closed, slide on and off.

He wanted to back away, run somewhere else. But where else could he run? He found himself frozen there, watching, like he was waiting for something to happen. Something terrible.

A hand reached out of a coffin. Then other hands stretched out of other coffins. Some looked like the hands of skeletons, while others were covered with leathery-looking flesh—flesh that fell off in flakes as the hands grabbed the sides of the boxes, pulling the rotting bodies up to look at Tad.

Tricks, these were all tricks, Tad reminded himself. He didn't have to believe any of them. None of them would scare him—ever.

Faces appeared above the coffins as the corpses sat up, one after another, all of them smiling at Tad, all of them leering at him with their death grins.

Then one of the corpses opened his mouth.

"We're waiting for you, boy," it said with a voice that sounded like a knife scraping across stone.

"We're waiting for you, Tad," another said in a whisper like a dying breeze. A third said the same thing, this one a rumble of thunder from an approaching storm.

Tad shook his head. They wouldn't take him. He'd run away again—somewhere—anywhere. But somehow his shoes wouldn't move; his feet seemed stuck to the floor.

And the corpses said something else.

"We're hungry, Tad. Oh so hungry."

"We're waiting for you."

"We're hungry. We're waiting."

Somehow he had to get away. He could make his feet move if he really wanted to. He had to look away, and run.

The corpses leaned forward in their coffins, as if they would all leap out at once, rushing forward to overwhelm Tad beneath a mountain of rotting flesh.

It was all tricks, he told himself. He would not be beaten by tricks.

He closed his eyes. And his feet moved. Once he could no longer see the corpses, the spell was broken.

He pulled himself away at last, and turned to run.

He opened his eyes, expecting to see the vacant hallway he had come through.

But someone was waiting for him there, too.

There, standing only a few feet away, watching him, were the young woman and the thin and nervous man from the music room. Edward, the thin man, still held the bloody knife. He moved forward quickly. The point of his knife pricked at Tad's throat.

"You'll come now," the man said.

He and the woman smiled at each other, like they were sharing their secret all over again. Tad looked down at the knife pressed to his throat.

The woman gasped. Edward made a gagging sound. The knife fell away from Tad.

Tad looked up and saw that someone had grabbed Edward by the neck. It was the old man Tad had seen in the game room, the only person thus far who hadn't wanted to use Tad as a prize.

The two men fought. Tad heard a great rustling noise behind him as the corpses all sat up. They watched and yelled and cheered as the two men struggled, like this was some sort of macabre wrestling match put on just for their amusement.

The old man threw the man with the knife against a stone wall.

Tad heard a crack. The knife slipped from Edward's hand.

Edward crumpled to the ground. He had stopped breathing. Maybe it was the light down here, but to Tad the man seemed to fade back into the shadows along the wall, as if he'd become some sort of statue there, like a stone carving of a corpse.

Tad, and the old man, turned to the woman.

She smiled apologetically, as if to say, surely, none of this was her fault. Her mouth opened, but not a single word came out.

Tad and the old man stood there for a long moment. And, as they watched, the woman changed.

Her body began to quiver, only a shudder at first, but soon she was shaking violently. And as she shook, she began to fall apart, as if she was made of something else besides bone and skin.

Holes popped open in her cheeks and hands, and thick greenish slime, oozed from the expanding wounds. Her apologetic grin twisted and turned.

A great tongue snaked out of her decomposing mouth, reaching out towards Tad, as if she would enwrap the boy with it and drag him down with her to death.

The old man stepped in front of Tad, ready to protect him, but the great long tongue fell heavily to the dusty floor, followed by the grotesque remnants of Martine Burden. Soon, all that remained of the woman was a greenish ooze, which seeped slowly into the earthen floor.

But Tad saw something in the ooze before it disappeared. A face, sneering up at him.

The old man gripped him by the shoulder. "You're okay, son. You're all right now. She's—it's—just an illusion."

But Tad didn't agree. Couldn't the old man see the face? It no longer belonged to the woman. Instead, it had turned into the face of the toymaker—Henry Stauf. And Stauf was laughing.

Tad was sure that the woman had really been there, and the woman had died, killed by Henry Stauf. As if the thin man and the woman were a single unit in Stauf's game, and, with one dead, the other one had to follow—as if they were all puppets for the mad toymaker.

The Stauf face laughed and winked at Tad, a wink that said, "See you soon."

Behind them, the corpses all shut themselves away, coffin lids slamming closed as if they could also see that face all too well.

"There's nothing else here," the old man said. He took Tad's hand and led him back the way he had come, out of the maze of the basement.

Tad looked up at the strange old man in the turban and cape. Maybe, with the old man's help, he might escape this house after all.

How could this have happened?

Dutton had had to let the others go. His knees were weak; he had to lean against a wall for support. He needed to rest a bit, that was all. Rest a bit, and then he would get about his business.

He had to find something to bind his wound. Once the bleeding stopped, he'd be fine. He'd have plenty of time to go to a hospital after he'd won Stauf's prize.

As soon as he'd taken care of his injury, he would go back to the chapel, ask the high priest for guidance. He had been the chosen one. Stauf's note had made that clear.

Stauf would not take away his reward, not when he was so close. Not when he was the chosen one. This was only a minor setback. Dutton was a survivor.

He left the music room, using the walls for support. He had to get back to his room. Perhaps a bit of rest on that nice, soft bed. There was probably a bathroom nearby, with some sort of first aid kit. If not, Dutton could always use the sheets to make a temporary bandage. Stauf wouldn't mind. After all, Dutton was the chosen one.

He leaned heavily against the railing as he slowly climbed the stairs. The door to his room was just across from the top of the stairs. Only a few more feet. Once inside his room, after a couple of deep breaths, Dutton pushed himself over to the bed.

The briefcase still sat there, the same case he had used to solve the puzzle that had led him to the chapel. He pushed it out of the way so that he might lie down. But, when his fingers brushed the leather case, they hit against the lock as well.

The case sprung open a couple of inches. Dutton saw a flash of green inside.

He pulled himself up to a sitting position and opened the case the rest of the way. It was filled with money, jam-packed with tens of thousands of dollar bills.

Dutton smiled. Stauf had given him his reward. It had been waiting here for him all along. There must be a million dollars in here.

He'd never have to worry about money again.

But he was having trouble keeping his eyes opened. It was this soft feather bed, surely. A bed fit for a king. King Dutton. He hadn't realized how tired he was.

He opened his eyes to look at the money one more time. His gaze slipped down to his shirt front, clinging-wet and a deep red-brown, drenched in blood.

He had forgotten about the wound. Where was all this blood coming from? It seemed like it would never stop.

He was having trouble sitting up. The money would give him strength. He reached down to pick up a few of the bills, but he couldn't feel his fingers.

Dutton managed to shake his head. This was all wrong. He was the survivor. He was the lucky one.

How could he bleed to death now, when he was rich?

He fell back on the bed, staring up at the ceiling.

He was very cold.

Before his eyes closed, Dutton found he was not at all surprised to see his own brother staring down at him, his face pressed against the ice.

Tad freed himself from the older man's grip. They were almost out of the basement, ready to go upstairs. But how far upstairs did the man want to take him?

"You have to come with me," the man with the turban said.

Tad looked up at him and, at the risk of seeming ungrateful, stated the obvious.

"Why should I trust you?" he asked.

Part of him wanted to be suspicious of everybody; it was this crazy house, where nothing was what it seemed. But even as Tad asked his question, he knew this man was different. Somehow, this man was worth trusting.

"Please," the old man insisted, but with a kindness in his eyes that Tad hadn't seen in the others. "Come with me. Before . . ."

He offered Tad his hand again. And Tad took it.

The old man looked up, sensing something but too late.

Tad looked up, too; he heard a high, thin whistle, the noise of something cutting through the air.

It was a wire, a thin, silvery wire whipping out of the darkness. It flashed across the hallway, over Tad's head, but at just the right height to slice the old man's neck.

Hamilton Temple let go of Tad's hand and reached up, trying to catch the wire before it cut his throat.

But he was too slow, his hand too late. The wire wrapped itself around Temple's neck. And, somewhere in the shadows above them, something pulled the wire taut with incredible force.

The old man gasped. His eyes bulged. He looked down at Tad, as if he was apologizing.

"No," Tad said, feeling the tears, even though he was fighting it. He started to cry. Like a baby. Like a wuss. The old man couldn't die. He was the only one who would help Tad.

"No, mister, please," Tad pleaded.

The wire pulled tighter still. Tad looked up. It was being pulled through a hole in the floor above. Another one of the toymaker's tricks.

The old man's eyes bulged out even more. He gasped. Tried to cough.

He slumped down, hanging from the wire. He stopped moving, then breathing.

The wire loosened. The old man slid to the floor.

Tad stood there, the body at his feet. He waited. He heard the door open to the basement. He heard the steps coming down.

The heavy footsteps.

He had nowhere else to go. He thought he heard the coffin lids open again behind him. The hungry corpses were waiting for him.

He could wait for the footsteps from above.

Or he could try to get by them.

THIRTY

Julia Heine had done just what Stauf wanted, setting up the wire to slit Temple as he passed— and the trick had worked like a charm. Temple was out of the way. Tad was alone and ready. Now she would get her reward.

She danced up to her room.

She looked in the mirror. She was old, but her wrinkles didn't look quite so bad in the soft candlelight. It made her remember the kind of reflection she once had seen.

"I once had beautiful hair," she announced.

She smiled at her reflection. Didn't her hair already seem to shine, like it had so many years ago? Perhaps her reward was beginning already.

"I once was young," she added, eager to help the process along.

Yes! The Julia in the mirror was getting younger. Her face was younger, more firm. The circles beneath her eyes, the crow's feet, her wrinkled brow, all vanished. Stauf knew what she wanted, and she would receive her reward!

"Oh, yes," she urged the mirror image. "Young. That's what I want. To be young again."

She spoke to the mirror as if she were talking to a lover. Coaxing the image, showing the way. She had given herself up totally to Stauf's will, and now Stauf would give to her. Yes! She had not felt this sense of elation, this total hope, in years. She would have a whole new future. She wouldn't make the same mistakes. She would leave the bottle and the bad men behind. She'd use her youth and beauty to get somewhere in the world.

She was so light on her feet!

"Why," she said with a coquettish smile, "I do appear to be free for this dance."

But the image in the mirror was growing younger still.

Perhaps even going too far.

She only wanted to be a young woman, in her twenties, a few years younger than Martine Burden. She didn't want to be too young. She had had such a difficult adolescence. All those things her father had done to her, and her mother wouldn't protect her. She didn't want to think about those things ever again.

"No, please." She shook her head. "This is too . . ."

But she was shrinking back into girlhood now, losing inches off her height. She couldn't think straight either, as if, as she lost her years, she was losing herself, as well.

Soon, she wouldn't remember anything, Julia realized with dawning horror. She would make the same mistakes all over again.

"No, this isn't what I wanted!" she shrieked. "This—"

She blinked. Why was she here? Why was she in this strange house. Had she done something wrong? Was Mommy punishing her again?

"No, Mommy! I want my mommy! I—"

But then she had forgotten how to talk. And to walk.

She was too small to see herself in the mirror, finally toppling out of the chair to crawl along the floor.. She crawled away from the mirror.

Somehow, she found herself in the hall.

She was Julia Heine again. Old Julia, all the youth gone.

Stauf could give her what she wanted. But she must be more specific. And there was more to be done.

She would find the boy and bring him to the toymaker. Maybe first, though, she would get herself a good, stiff drink.

She had learned her lesson at the mirror. This was her last mistake.

When she finally met Stauf face to face, she would tell him exactly what she needed.

Tad couldn't face the coffins again. So he decided to face whoever, or whatever, was coming for him. He was young and he could run. Maybe he could slip past the approaching footsteps and reach the first floor.

He had taken only a few steps leading out of the basement when he froze, blinking his eyes in disbelief.

He was no longer in the basement.

Instead, he was at the top of another set of stairs, looking out at a room he'd never seen before. It was a room higher up than he had ever been, farther up than the second floor. Somehow, Stauf had brought him all the way upstairs.

Tad started to cry. How could he get away if the toymaker could change the very house around him, so that when he stepped one place he landed somewhere else?

But there was farther to go. He hadn't gotten all the way to Stauf yet. Maybe he could try to run downstairs again. Maybe he could find some way out of this place yet.

He turned to the stairs and met an old woman coming towards him.

The old woman smiled.

Somehow, Julia Heine had known enough to walk up the stairs, rather than going down. Stauf was helping her now, showing her the way. One hand washes the other, she guessed. She walked up to the third floor and there was her prize, only a few feet away.

She looked down at the boy, cowering at the top of the stairs. Such a sweet-looking face. Such a nice-looking boy.

She reached down and caressed his cheek. It was wet. He was crying.

"No," she said. "There's nothing to be scared of. Come, tell me. What's your name?"

The boy kept crying, but he answered her.

"T-tad."

It would be so difficult for one so young. He would never understand the needs of his elders. Or what Stauf needed to sacrifice him for. How badly Julia needed that reward. If she had her youth again, she would know what to do with it.

He was such a poor boy, so young, so stupid. She would end his pain.

She took Tad's hand and pulled the boy up. "Come with me, sweetheart." She pulled the boy to a standing position.

It would all be over quickly. She would guide him now, to Henry Stauf and her reward.

THIRTY-ONE

ad gave her his hand. He didn't know what else to do.

He had seen this woman once before, in the kitchen, sorting cans. She had acted a little crazy then, totally absorbed by what she was doing.

Tad wondered how crazy she was now.

She was an old woman. She even looked a little like his grandmother. She wouldn't hurt him, would she?

She tugged at Tad's hand, leading him across the attic. The half-finished toys and other junk were scattered everywhere, and they had to pick their way between the piles.

Tad still wasn't sure he wanted to come along. He had always been taught to respect his elders, but he couldn't forget what his mother told him about what bad people could do to kids.

"Where are we going?" He tried to pull his hand away, but the woman held onto his wrist so firmly that it almost hurt. "Where are you taking me?"

She smiled down at him, a kindly grandmother sort of smile.

"It's okay, honey." Her tone was very quiet, very sweet. "Everything's fine now. You're safe. You're with me. Everything's fine."

She went on and on. Somehow, Tad thought, she sounded *too* sweet.

The room looked very strange in front of them, as if one whole side of the house was shimmering. In a weird sort of way, Tad decided the air in front of them looked the way a frog looked, glistening with water, right after you pulled it out of a pond.

If they passed through that shimmering surface, there would be no going back. Tad was sure of that.

But how did he know?

He heard a noise, like the whimper of some wounded animal. Something was hurt, hiding somewhere up in the attic.

Like this woman could hurt him.

This was all wrong. The lady was moving him too fast. He dug in his heels and tried to stop their rush through the room.

"What was that?" he demanded.

"Nothing, dear," the woman said without even looking down at him. "We have to be going." Toys scattered as she dragged him forward. "Everything's fine. You're with me."

But he had heard something, a sad, whimpering sound, made by something that had no hope left in the world.

And the noise grew. It echoed through the attic until the whole house was moaning.

A woman's voice was making the noise, a different woman from the one who held Tad. This voice sounded every bit as afraid as he felt.

He turned his head to either side. The voice was coming from somewhere among all the piles of toys, but the way noise echoed up here, it was hard to tell just where.

"Hello?" Tad called out.

"Help me," the frightened voice replied. "Please, some-one help me—"

Tad tried to stop again, but the old woman still wouldn't let him go. He decided he'd had enough of this oh-so-kindly lady with the iron grip. If she really wanted to help him, she would have wanted to help the woman, too. She was too sweet on the surface, and not sweet at all underneath, like the witch in that old nursery story about Hansel and Gretel.

He couldn't get anywhere trying to pull away, so Tad jumped forward and kicked the old woman in the shins. She let go of him with a yelp.

Tad jumped away. Maybe he could find the second woman and free her from the mounds of toys. Maybe they could get away together.

The old lady circled around him and blocked his way to the stairs going down. She didn't look sweet anymore; the kick in the leg had made her angry.

Tad darted left. He was closer to the voice now, to someone calling out over and over.

"Help me. Please. I can't move. I need help—"

He was almost on top of the voice. Tad burrowed into the pile of toys, pushing aside broken puzzles and dolls without heads and wheel-less trucks and—

He saw someone at the edge of the pile.

A woman's face poked through the discarded toys.

She opened her mouth.

"Help me."

He frowned as he looked at her. Her face was fine, but something was wrong with her body. Like maybe she was strapped to sticks of wood, like the arms and legs of a big marionette.

He scooped broken toys out of the way, hoping to free the woman, to get her out of whatever weird harness trapped her.

The woman looked right at Tad. "Something's wrong with me. I looked over here, and—"

Tad looked down again as he threw the final toys off her body. She wasn't tied to wooden poles. Those were her real arms and legs, or what her arms and legs had become, nothing more than long, wooden sticks. Her head was human, but her whole body looked like brightly-painted, highly-polished wood.

She was turning into a toy, like some kind of giant puppet. Tad felt suddenly cold, as if a winter breeze had pushed through this stifling attic. The last adult who could help him was turning into a piece of wood.

"I can't move," she cried.

But what could he do?

Tad shook his head and smiled sadly. Part of him wanted to scream at the sight of this—a woman turning into a piece of wood. But he was almost beyond being scared. Besides, it wouldn't do him any good. Not now. He had to get away.

Or he had to spit right in Henry Stauf's eye.

He looked up and saw a dusty mirror. A strange mirror, decorated with curls and spirals and small, eye-like dots.

Hadn't he seen that mirror before?

He muttered an apology to the wooden lady and turned away. Somehow, it was very important that he look into that mirror. He jumped over a smaller pile of toys and positioned himself in front of it. He stared in the glass.

But the glass showed nothing but darkness. If this was really a mirror, it showed another time, or another place.

There was magic all around him: the wooden lady, the shimmering air, this strange mirror. If only he could learn to use it, too. Then he'd show Old Man Stauf a few things.

He heard toys scatter behind him. The other lady was after him again. He looked for somewhere to run, but the magic mirror was pushed close to a corner, with even larger piles of junk to either side. The only way out of here was the way he'd come.

He turned around to see the older woman almost on top of him. He jumped forward and tried to run around her.

And she grabbed him, so firmly now that her hands felt like claws. She pulled him toward the door at the far end of the attic.

"Come here," she said, her sweet, reassuring voice turned into a growl. "Come here, you little—"

Her face was twisted in anger, her body rigid with hate. Tad was so overwhelmed by the change in her that he forgot to struggle for a moment.

They passed through the shimmering cloud. Tad looked around him. Everything on this side of that glowing curtain glistened, as if it had just been touched with morning dew.

The woman flung the door open so hard that it smashed against the wall. With Tad still locked in her grip, she started to climb.

There was no going back now. Stauf waited for them at the end of a final flight of stairs.

THIRTY-TWO

He knows what has to be done.

He hears the voices ahead of him. It is time to climb the stairs to the attic.

He takes them quickly, and finds himself on the third floor. Broken toys are scattered everywhere, just as he expected. He hears a clatter on the far side of the room. The old lady is still dragging the boy upstairs. He has a minute before the final confrontation.

He picks his way through the piles of debris. There is another noise close by, a mumbling sound, as though someone is trying to talk through a gag.

He sees, lying on the floor, a woman. Or at least what was once a woman. Stauf's power has changed her, turning her torso, arms and legs to polished wood. The shape of her head changes as he looks down at her, becoming rounder, with painted apple cheeks. Her hair transforms into tight wooden curls.

She seems to see him, too. Her lips, still somehow human, manage the slightest of smiles.

Even with the changes, he recognizes her. It is Elinor Knox. The name pops into his head. Maybe he knows the names of all the guests.

Elinor's skin has turned hard and shiny. Her eyes are bright and blue, as if they were marbles set in her head. He is surprised she can see anything at all.

"I knew you would come back," she says.

He has been here before, many times. So she knows this, too?

"I cannot stay long," he replies. But perhaps she knows that as well.

She has trouble talking. Her mouth creaks as she speaks, as if her jaw is built on hinges.

"Oh, of course," she manages, and the creaking grows louder with every word. "How silly of me. You're the other one." Her bright blue eyes shift toward the far end of the attic, as if she wants to look up the stairs to Stauf's lair. "I can't save him anymore. But you can."

"Yes," he agrees, and realizes that that was his purpose all along. He glances toward the final set of stairs. The voices of the woman and the boy are more distant now. He will have to hurry.

He turns back to Elinor Knox, only to see that her transformation is complete. Her face is frozen. Where once there was a moving mouth, there is nothing now but a wooden smile. Somehow, though, he feels she might have had a different expression if he had not been here.

Now he will go on upstairs, and make that smile mean something.

He stands up. There, immediately in front of him is a mirror, quite a fancy standing mirror, the frame decorated with curls and spirals, and small, eye-like dots.

Something draws him to the looking glass. It will only take a moment, and it feels very important.

He steps carefully in front of it, avoiding the broken toys that litter this place. At first, the image in the mirror is dark. But then colors shift within the darkness. They are blurry for an instant, but then an image takes form.

It is an image he never expected.

THIRTY-THREE

This was going so well, Henry Stauf wanted to applaud. Everything was marching along according to plan, his guests dying right on schedule and, when possible, in the most demeaning ways imaginable. Stauf took pride in his work, after all.

Look at his accomplishments so far. He was especially proud of the mundane death of Hamilton Temple, as far away from magic as he could get; and yet strangulation with a wire had a certain Oriental flair. Stauf thought of it as his own personal Indian Rope Trick.

And the others. Poor Edward Knox, overreaching himself until he broke his back. Brian Dutton dying with all the money he had ever wanted in his grasp, but now far beyond his ability to spend. And dear Martine Burden, who had sealed her fate when she tried to get someone else to take responsibility for her actions. In Henry Stauf's mansion, everyone was responsible. When her new partner Edward died, well, she had to share the blame. And the death.

Each had gotten what was most fitting.

Of course a few of his guests weren't entirely dead.

He'd kept Elinor Knox—well, not quite alive—but she'd never be able to do anything for herself again. He couldn't think of a better marionette.

Now it was down to Julia Heine and the boy.

And the boy, dear Tad, was reserved for the voices. The final piece of their bargain. The final blood that would set them free.

Stauf wanted to laugh and laugh. But he had other business to attend to.

He could hear them on the stairs.

THIRTY-FOUR

e looks in the mirror. And a boy looks back at him. Tad Gorman stares at him, face to face.

For an instant, he thinks the mirror is playing tricks.

But no. The mirror is showing his true image after all.

"I've been here before," he whispers. "I've seen all this. Over and over—"

"Help me!" Tad says from the other side of the mirror. "Please."

He reaches out and touches the mirror with his finger. On the other side, Tad has moved his finger forward to touch the same spot on the glass, finger to finger.

But the finger doesn't feel like it is touching glass. Instead, he feels like he is touching another hand. Even if that hand might be another part of himself.

"Tried to help him," he says softly, or perhaps he only thinks it. "Tried to help—myself. Always failing. Always—"

He hears a woman's voice call out from the upstairs.

"You little bastard!"

As soon as he hears the words, he knows it is Julia Heine's voice. And Tad—or himself—has slipped away for a minute.

It is time. He has to go. Maybe this time it will work.

Only he can change everything.

THIRTY-FIVE

ulia Heine dragged the boy up the last of the stairs, and to a small, garret room at the very top of the house.

There, in the middle of the darkened chamber, sat Henry Stauf.

He sat, unmoving, hunched over in a wheelchair. He did nothing to acknowledge their presence. Julia wondered if he might be asleep. Even in the dim light of the garret, she could see how decrepit he had become. She never thought he would be so old.

Julia felt an instant of doubt. If he had the power over life and death, why didn't he use it on himself?

But then, perhaps Mr. Stauf had other things on his mind. Perhaps his power wasn't complete until he had the boy.

And he had promised Julia her heart's desire.

Stauf shifted in his chair. He looked up slowly, as if any movement was a great effort. He glanced at the boy, then turned his gaze to Julia.

"Bring him here," he demanded.

Oh, of course. Julia dragged the boy in front of her. Seeing Stauf in person like this, for the first time, had startled her a bit. She had come this far for a purpose. She should at least complete her side of the bargain.

To be young again! She thought about the promise offered her in the bedroom mirror. She almost giggled as she handed over the boy.

"I brought him," she chattered eagerly. "The one you wanted. The guest. I—"

The little bastard started to struggle again.

Even now, he was trying to get away. Didn't he know it was hopeless?

"No!" he screamed, every muscle in his thin frame pulling against her. "Please. Somebody, help!"

She yanked the boy roughly forward, pushing him toward Stauf. She'd be glad just to get the little hellion out of her hands.

Couldn't the boy see that he had lost?

He rushes upstairs and sees the scene unfold before him; a scene he remembers all too well.

He steps into the garret room. The place is cramped, ill-lit, and, if possible, more of a ruin than any other room in the house. The smell of this place is overpowering, rancid and vile, a mixture of acid and rot.

He forgets about the room, the smell, everything—when he looks at Tad.

"I'm that boy," he says aloud. Nobody in the room turns when he speaks. Apparently, they cannot hear him. At this moment, neither of the others matters.

He can't take his eyes off the boy, feeling himself to be the man that Tad will become. But Tad will only grow to be a man if Stauf can be stopped.

Can Stauf be stopped? That is the only question that counts, the reason he is in this room.

And he is here, the man Tad will become. Perhaps that is the answer already. Whatever he is, whether the boy's future, the boy's spirit, the hope of the human race, maybe just the hand of fate—there is no time to question his true purpose. No doubt he's done that in the past, and it has cost Tad's life.

His life.

He risks a moment to look around—and to remember. Things are different in this garret. Somehow all the physical laws are changed. Past, present, maybe even future can all exist together.

Stauf has changed the nature of time and space in this house. The man who once was Tad has seen it in the puzzles, the tricks, and the way he has made people die. Nowhere is that power stronger than here, in Stauf's lair, at the very pinnacle of the house.

If the man can understand it, he can use it to his—and Tad's—advantage.

But how can he use all this to defeat Stauf? The others in the room cannot see or hear him, and he looks through all of them in turn, as if they are ghosts as well.

Tad screams as he is pushed toward Stauf.

"No! Let me go!"

Stauf's mouth opens slightly, and a snake-like tongue darts in and out to taste the air, as if he was searching for flies.

Julia is oblivious to it all. A smile fills her ancient face. Her feet skip across the rotten floorboards like dance steps. She pushes Tad forward so that he is only a few feet away from the wheelchair-bound Stauf.

"My wish," she calls in a happy sing-song. "I'll get my wish."

Stauf smiles at that, a smile so large that it looks like his gums might wither away, leaving nothing but yellow, half-rotted teeth.

His mouth opens wide. He vomits.

A great mass of thick, green, viscous fluid falls to the floor. It slides across the rotting wood, encircling Julia Heine's feet like something alive.

Julia begins to sink into the fluid at her feet.

"No," she cries in disbelief. "What are you—"

She slaps at the floor, but the green pool catches her hands and sucks them down hungrily.

It is Julia's turn to struggle, now. Except that her every movement only seems to make her sink more quickly

"No, no, you promised," she shouts at the silent Stauf. "You cheated me!"

Now it is her turn to scream. Except her screams are soon lost beneath the bubbling ooze.

Tad stares for an instant at the place where Julia Heine disappeared. The green liquid is seeping into the floorboards. Another moment, and it is gone.

Tad turns and backs away from Stauf. But the boy is too close to the madman. Tad's future self, if that's what he is, remembers what comes next.

"Run!" he calls anyway. "Run, for God's sake!"

Tad looks toward his older counterpart, but there is no recognition in his eyes.

The older Tad opens his mouth again to call out, but any sound is overwhelmed by a sudden, maddening flurry of voices. Screaming.

Stauf's mouth opens again. His tongue snakes out, fantastically long, and wraps itself around Tad.

Tad screams as Stauf's tongue lifts him from the floor and snaps the boy back to Stauf's lap, like some lizard reeling in its dinner. Stauf opens his mouth, wider, then wider still. It is time to feed.

The wheelchair moves back into darkness.

The house begins to rumble. The walls pulsate, in and out, as if the whole room is breathing. The walls take on a light of their own, glowing as small growths erupt upon their faces. The growths spread and elongate, unfurling into great tendrils that reach out, as if sensing the presence of one last victim that will make the spell complete.

"No!" the man Tad might become cries as he backs down the stairs. "What is happening? What is—"

But the noise of the house and the voices is so loud now that he cannot even hear his own screams. The glowing walls sprout what at first look like cracks. But then he realizes the walls have turned translucent. The lines are inside the walls, and really look more like veins. He sees flashes of events that have happened elsewhere in the house—the stabbing in the music room, the ghost in the soup pot, the corpses in the basement. And a hundred dolls calling out with a hundred voices—as if time and space no longer have any meaning.

The tendrils are still growing all around him, threatening to fill the attic with their great, pulpy mass, a cancer gone wild. Some of the tendrils thicken, become tentacles that reach for him, while others sprout the heads of children, calling out to him in a language he cannot understand. The noise is deafening, and grows louder with every second.

Somehow, in the midst of the madness, one voice, calls out above the others. Tad's voice.

"Help me!"

Then it is two voices, young and old, calling together.

"Help me! Help me!"

And then there are more than two. The voice of Elinor Knox has joined with them—Elinor Knox, whose face has turned to wood, but who somehow cries out in his brain.

"Help me!"

But Elinor Knox is not alone. Behind her, he realizes, there are a hundred voices more, voices high and strident and full of need.

"Help me!" they cry. And he realizes they are the voices of the dolls, the spirits of the children! Somehow, they have reached through Elinor to join them here.

Then, as abruptly as it began, the crushing wall of noise ceases, and all is darkness.

And then the world changes—again.

Tad wouldn't let them get him! He would struggle, he would bite and kick and scratch until the lady let him go!

"No! I want to get out of here!"

She dragged him up the stairs to the final room. She didn't care about him at all. She was one of those bad people that his mother and warned him about.

And Henry Stauf, the toymaker, was another one.

The woman pulled Tad around in front of her, so that he could see the old man in the wheelchair. Tad almost stumbled as she pushed him forward.

"My wish!" the old lady cried out before him, her voice sounding as giddy as a little girl's. "I'll get my wish."

Tad looked at her with the dawning realization that she had completely lost her mind.

Suddenly, something came out of Stauf's mouth, a glob of something green and vile that flowed deliberately around the old lady's feet.

The lady started to sink down inside it.

"No. What are you—" She struggled, but it sucked her in like quicksand. Worse than quicksand. It looked like it was dragging her down, like it was hungry.

"No," the lady screamed. "No—you promised—you cheated me!"

Her words were cut off as her head sank into the gooey liquid. Tad looked up at Stauf. He had to get out of here.

"Run!" somebody called. "For God's sake—"

Who was that? Was there somebody else up here?

Tad knew that voice, and needed no encouragement.

He turned to run, only to have his first stride cut short.

Something wrapped itself around Tad's middle, jerking him off his feet and pulling him back towards Stauf.

"Please," Tad called out desperately. "Please, help me."

Tad could hear horrible sucking sounds coming from behind him, coming from Stauf. And there was a rumbling coming from somewhere else, as if the whole house would shake apart.

Tad still had one hand free, and with it he reached out. Someone else was there; someone who could help.

"Please help me!" he called.

And the voice answered, much louder than before:

"No, by God. No. You can't have him."

Tad saw a hand, glowing in the air before him.

"You can't have me!"

The glow spread and opened, and Tad saw a strangely familiar young man standing before him.

The young man reached forward, and their fingers touched. They clasped hands. Tad could feel warmth and strength flowing from the other's fingers.

The young man was not alone. Behind him, Tad could see the smiling faces of a hundred dolls. But when he looked again he realized they weren't dolls after all, but a hundred smiling children.

Tad had the feeling this had happened before, with he and Stauf and the young man in the attic room. But this time was different. This time all the children would help them.

Tad felt Stauf's grip loosen on his body. He spun away, and saw that the old man was changing. His skin shriveled upon his face and hands, drying and flaking until the bones showed through. Then the bones crumbled as well, and the wheelchair beneath him, and all the strange new things that had begun to grow in this room—all of it just crumbled into dust.

Tad couldn't help himself. He was crying. But he was smiling, too.

"You saved me," he whispered to the young stranger. "You—"

But a bright glow had filled the entire room, taking Tad's words away. The sun had risen outside, and light poured through every opening, all the windows around them, and the skylight up above.

"It's all changed," Tad said. But he somehow felt that the young man, so familiar yet so strange, was speaking along with him. "It's over now. Now and . . ."

"Forever," the other man finished for him. And to the boy Tad it seemed as if the familiar stranger actually became the light, glowing then fading as the sun poured into the room.

The sun grew brighter still, until Tad's whole world was filled with white.

Somewhere, in the distance, he could hear the sound of a hundred children, laughing.

About the Authors

Matthew J. Costello, a novelist who also contributes to such diverse magazines as *Amazing Stories*, *Games Magazine*, and *Sports Illustrated*, is the author of *The Time Warrior* novels *Time of the Fox* and *Hour of the Scorpion*, the *SeaQuest DSV* novel *Fire Below*, and the novels *Homecoming* and *See How She Runs*. He wrote the original screenplay for *The 7th Guest* and its sequel, *The 11th Hour.*

* * *

Craig Shaw Gardner is the author of *The Other Sinbad*, *The Ebenezum Trilogy*, *The Cineverse Cycle*, and many other works of fiction. His book *Dragon Sleeping*, the first of *The Dragon Circle*, was called, "One of the three outstanding fantasy novels of 1994," by *Science Fiction Chronicle*. He also wrote the movie novelizations of both *Batman* and *Batman Returns*, the former a *New York Times* bestseller.